8

Broken Ferns

A Lei Crime Novel

Broken Ferns

A Lei Crime Novel

Toby Neal

ISBN 978-0-9839524-9-7

Photo credit: Mike Neal © Nealstudios.net
Cover Design: © JULIE METZ LTD.

Book design by Mythic Island Press LLC

Proverbs 4:23:

Above all else, guard your heart,

for it is the wellspring of life.

Chapter 1

*I*t was a beautiful day to steal an airplane.

Special Agent Leilani Texeira put her hands on her hips and scanned the wide-open bay of the vast steel storage building Paradise Airlines owner Max Smiley used as a hangar and big-boy toy box. Her partner, Ken Yamada, photographed the area: smooth cement floor dotted with a few drops of oil where the ultralight plane had been parked. Ceiling-mounted racks of already-rigged windsurf sails hung above a row of quad vehicles and dirt bikes, all neatly parked in metal stanchions. Along the far wall, a row of shiny antique roadsters gleamed.

"It should be right here." Smiley's caterpillar-thick gray brows were drawn together into a single untrimmed hedgerow over narrowed blue eyes. He stamped his foot for emphasis. "Right here."

Lei walked to the door opening, a rolling garage-style retracted up on a track in the ceiling. The weather was perfect for flying, sunny and still. A blacktopped landing strip merged seamlessly with the floor of the steel barn. The narrow airstrip was edged with tasteful palms and bird-of-paradise, and a series of volcanic-rock stepping stones wound to the turquoise sea. Lei felt the sun, softer in the humid Kaneohe area of Oahu, beating on the top of her curly head. She fished mirrored aviators out of her pocket, slipped them on as she turned back to Smiley.

"You said the house is clear?"

"He got in while we were sleeping. I went through the house when I saw what he did, then came out here."

"Do you always leave this unlocked?" She indicated the hasp of the sectioned door, hanging free and unmarked.

"Yeah. I've got a locked security gate and the fence goes to the beach. Theft hasn't been a problem in this area. But whoever did this knew about aircraft and flew my plane right out of here, goddamn it!" Smiley's full face got redder. "You can bet I'm going to lock it from now on. Come see what he did to the house."

Lei looked over at Ken, who was finishing up with a couple of shots of the open door of the hangar. "We'll come back and dust for prints," he said, walking beside Smiley as the mogul led the way to the huge beach house that sprawled against a grassy knoll. "We'll need pictures of the aircraft and any other identifying information you can give us."

The house was done in a classic island style, and Lei couldn't help but like the wide, deep roofline that sheltered a porch that ran the length and breadth of the house. The lanai was dotted with Adirondack chairs in weathered cedar, pointed toward the stunning view of beach and sky.

"How the other one percent lives," she muttered in aside to Yamada.

Smiley advanced to a bank of glass sliders that fronted the house and pushed one open. Inside, glossy tile covered by woven lauhala matting ended at a stainless-steel modern kitchen. He made a dramatic gesture.

"Look at this!" he exclaimed. "He's taunting me!"

Bold block printing—probably Sharpie—in a street-graffiti style decorated the shiny steel refrigerator.

YOU STOLE FROM ME.

NOW I'M STEALING FROM YOU.

HAOLE.

The Hawaiian word for Caucasian, not a complimentary sentiment, was followed by a smiley face. Ken lifted the Canon 7D, soundlessly clicking away as Lei took a little spiral notebook out of the pocket of her slacks.

"I wonder if that drawing is about your name, or if it means something else. Have you seen this graffiti anywhere at Paradise Air? Do you have any ideas who could be involved?"

"Maybe." Smiley reached for the door of the fridge.

Lei waved him back. "We need to get prints off there, too."

"I already opened it before. He took some food." Smiley withdrew his hand. "I think it was one of my employees. I've gotten some hate mail lately. I already told all this to the police officers that first came."

"I'm sorry for the repetition, sir. The case was bumped to the Bureau due to the stolen aircraft aspect and your high profile as the company's owner. We'll need to take a look at any and all negative correspondence you have," Ken said.

A woman burst into the room from a bedroom suite off to the left. Lei's hand fell to her weapon at the intrusion.

"Max, Angel's missing! I'm looking everywhere and I can't find her!"

"Is this a kidnapping now?" Lei asked Smiley, whose ruddy face had gone pale.

"It might as well be," he growled, embracing the distraught woman who'd flung herself into his arms. "Angel's our dog. Chihuahua. She's our baby."

"Well, shit, it could be worse," Lei said, even as her heart squeezed, remembering her Rottweiler, Keiki. Ken shot her a quelling glance, but it was too late.

"It couldn't be worse, goddamn it," Smiley bawled. "Some asshole broke into my house and stole my plane and my dog! Find the sonofabitch, and find him now!"

Lei felt the blush that had always been her undoing in the tingling of her scalp, a pink wave of color moving up her olive-skinned, freckled face. Somehow in her mixed heritage of Hawaiian, Japanese, and Portuguese, the outspoken, impulsive *Portagee* part was what always got her in trouble.

And though she'd said it could be worse, she knew the pain of losing a dog firsthand.

Even in the heat, Ken's gray summer-weight FBI suit hung in perfect lines from his chiseled frame as he moved to stand beside her. His stern face projected authority and competence.

"Calm down, sir. We're at the very beginning of the investigation. I'm sure we'll be able to track down your plane and dog in short order. Why don't you and your wife take a break while we do a walk-through, see what we can see? You two can make us a list of what you know is missing."

Smiley pulled his wife over onto the couch, looped a hamlike arm over her. She was still in her nightgown, the old-fashioned kind with a tucked neckline, thin cotton printed in sprigs of roses. A jumble of silver-blond hair spilled over his hands as he patted her back and muttered gruff, soothing noises into her ear as she cried on his neck.

Emmeline Smiley appeared to have been hit hard by the burglary, or at least by the loss of the dog. Lei felt a little pang as she turned to Ken. "Where first?"

"Wherever there might be something worth stealing." Ken addressed Smiley. "Do you have a home safe?"

Smiley pointed down the hallway his wife had entered from. Lei and Ken headed toward it, Lei, as the junior agent, trailing slightly behind. They kept their hands on their weapons and checked each opulent room.

Several bedrooms, each more luxurious than the last, opened off the short hall. A pair of double doors bisected the end of the passageway, and Ken pulled one door open while Lei turned into the room, weapon in "low ready" position, finger alongside the trigger, aimed down and away from her partner.

Empty.

The room was traditionally furnished: green-shaded lawyer's lamp over a burled-wood desk, thick red carpet, a gas fireplace, and a pair of leather recliners fronting a flatscreen TV. A pool table and a wet bar completed the male sanctuary.

The two agents moved into the room. Double French doors (locked, Lei checked, pushing down lightly with a tissue from the desk) faced out to the ever-present ocean view. A large oil painting, a front view of the beach house, hung on the wall behind the desk.

"Seems a likely spot." Ken reholstered his sidearm, carefully lifted the painting off the wall with tissues. Lei inspected the shiny steel surface of the wall safe, her tilted brown eyes reflecting back as her straight brows pulled together in concentration. She touched the dial with a tissue. It didn't budge.

"Still locked."

They rejoined the couple in the living room, where Smiley produced a file folder on the ultralight. Ken handed Lei the photos of the aircraft after he inspected them. Lei frowned. It was a sleek, chrome-colored shape, every inch a miniature airplane, with a propeller, a twenty-five-foot wingspan, tiny wheels, and a Plexiglas bubble over the cockpit.

"This looks like a real plane," she said. "I thought ultralights were more like bicycles with wings. Does it run on special fuel?"

"The Hummel is a kit. I built it myself. And no, it runs on

ordinary gasoline." Apparently, for twenty thousand dollars, the kit could be ordered online and shipped right to anyone's home.

They left for the FBI main office in Honolulu in the Bureau's black Acura SUV after issuing a Be on Lookout for a missing ultralight aircraft: one sleek silver Hummel Ultracruiser, Model H-3443. Also missing were half a ham, a loaf of bread, six hundred dollars in cash left out for the housekeeper to do the shopping, and one teacup Chihuahua named Angel.

Chapter 2

*T*his could get interesting," said Lei, sorting the stack of hate mail Smiley had given them into chronological order as Ken drove back to the Bureau headquarters in Honolulu. Stowed behind her seat was a crime kit filled with various samples and fingerprint slides and photographs of the plane and the dog.

"One thing about the Bureau. Nothing's ever boring." Lei knew Ken had ten years at the Bureau, paired with her for his strong closure rate and adherence to protocol—Special Agent in Charge Waxman had apparently heard rumors about Lei's rule-bending ways.

Lei liked that Ken had been recruited out of Columbia as an undergrad but had grown up in Hawaii and was able to "blend," using pidgin when it helped a case. As a native to Hawaii, too, she had some of the same advantages but came from a much rougher background.

This whole FBI thing was Marcella's fault, Lei thought as she sorted the stack of letters. Special Agent Marcella Scott, whom she'd met on one of her cases as a police officer, had become a friend and had been the one to recruit her to the Bureau. Not a day went by that Lei didn't wonder if she'd made the right decision.

One hand crept into her pocket, and she withdrew the round metal talisman she always carried—a bit of hammered, melted white gold embedded with a roughness of diamonds. She rubbed it, thinking of faces she'd loved and lost.

Ken glanced over. "What's that?"

"Ancient history."

He cocked an eyebrow. "Spill." They'd been paired for only a few weeks, and there were a lot of gaps in the story she'd told him when they first met.

"Why?"

"Partners. Gotta know the good, the bad, and the ugly. So I know how to look out for you, and vice versa."

"You first."

"Okay. Only child. Attended Punahou. Favorite color is FBI blue."

"Pfft. That's all in the bio. Gimme a real secret. So I know you trust me like you're asking me to trust you."

A long moment passed. Finally, "I'm gay." His warrior's face looked out the window, turned away from her.

"Damn. My gaydar's usually pretty good and it totally missed you." She said it with a smile.

"I'm with the Bureau. Last frontier of 'don't ask, don't tell.'"

"Okay, then. I still have a touch of PTSD from my past—abused as a kid. It acts up sometimes. This helps." She held up the disc.

"What is it?" Ken reached for it, but she put it back in her pocket.

"Just a gift from a friend." Lei wasn't ready for quite that much disclosure. "So, what do you think about our burglar?"

"What do you think?" Ken was still testing her, checking her reasoning.

"Might be a kid, or an adult trying to seem like one. Probably not a crime of opportunity, because most burglars wouldn't know how to fly that ultralight. With the graffiti, it looks like the Smileys were targeted. Someone's got an ax to grind—and some impulse-control problems, evidenced by the grabbing of the dog."

Ken inclined his head in agreement. "I bet we find something in the hate mail. This unsub's got exposure to aircraft, probably either an employee or family member of an employee. What do you think the smiley face means?"

Lei thought about the scribbled symbol. "Let me look at the photos." She reached back and picked up the Canon, scrolled through the photos of the scene and magnified the one of the graffiti. "The mouth isn't actually smiling. It's kind of got a hook at the end."

"We'll go over everything at the station and I can take a good look again. I remember that, though. It's not exactly a smile. What about the *haole* tagline?"

"Either he's a local or trying to seem like one. Could actually be Caucasian and trying to throw us off."

They pulled up at the downtown Prince Kuhio Federal Building, entering the underground garage. Ken ran their keycard across the scanner, which allowed them to pass a guard box. A few minutes later, they rose in the elevator to the tenth floor, where the Bureau had its offices.

Lei had spent her first four months in the Bureau at Quantico, Virginia, doing intensive training and the last six months on New Agent Trainee probation. During that time, she'd run background checks and done interviews of applicants to the Bureau, interspersed with grunt work at various field offices around the country before this posting, the one Marcella had set her up for.

She was finally feeling a little more comfortable in the relatively posh building after years as a police officer in a variety of well-worn headquarters. The FBI office's glossy setting, with marble floors, leather seating, a coffee table, and a receptionist in a bulletproof booth, still felt way too slick. She and Ken lifted a hand to the receptionist—actually a NAT, as she had recently been. They ran keycards across another scanner, and the interior doors, stainless steel behind faux wood paneling, whooshed open.

Lei's black athletic shoes squeaked as they walked down the hall, the sound a marked contrast to the *tippety-tap* of Marcella's heels as her friend hurried out of her office.

"Lei! I hear you guys pulled the Smiley burglary—I wanted that one!"

"She's got to cut her teeth on something, and it looks like an easy one," Ken said.

"I'm still not over running into you every day," Marcella said to Lei, a smile lighting her face as she fisted hands on hips. The senior agent always looked as if she'd stepped off the cover of *Vogue*—the severe FBI "uniform" somehow enhancing a curvy figure, golden tan, and tiny waist. The only nonregulation thing Marcella always wore were glamour shoes—today's were pointy-toed slingbacks.

Lei pushed her curly, frizzing hair back, a marked contrast to Marcella's smooth, dark updo. Ken went on to their office with the crime kits and camera.

"It's great being in the same building, at least—and this case is interesting. It's nice to get away from all those applicant screenings they had me doing during probation."

"Ken's a good partner for you. He'll keep you honest, show you the ropes." Marcella gave Lei's arm a little tug, pulling her into the spare little cubicle she shared with her partner, Matt Rogers. "Got a minute?"

"Just a minute. Ken's going to want to go over all the evidence we collected, get our casework started."

"Okay. So—have you heard from Stevens?"

Lei blushed for the second time that day, a crimson wave. Even though Marcella knew all there was to know about her bumpy love life with Detective Michael Stevens on Maui, she couldn't suppress the reaction to his name. Her hand slid into her pocket, rubbing the white-gold disc.

"No. I told you we broke up when I left. We haven't stayed in touch. He told me he wasn't waiting for me when I left for the Academy. It's been a year now, and I've been waiting for the right time to...look him up."

Stevens was her first love, and they'd been living together on Maui when she left him to join the FBI, a move that had seemed a fatal parting of the ways—but things had worked out as she'd hoped, and postprobation, she'd been posted in Honolulu. She'd been procrastinating, hoping for a good excuse to call him.

"Maybe you shouldn't bother." Something in Marcella's voice made Lei snap her head up to look at her friend. Marcella's strong-boned face was set, her full mouth a tight line and arched brows pulled together in a frown. "He's married."

"What?" Lei felt the blood drain out of her face. Her vision telescoped, black encroaching around a circle that centered on one of Marcella's concerned brown eyes. *It's the PTSD—breathe,* she told herself. Her fingers curled, pinching her thigh through the light fabric of her slacks, hard, and pain grounded her. She sucked in a breath. "What did you say?"

"He's married." Marcella reached into the small refrigerator beside her desk, splashed water from a filtration carafe into a wax-paper cup, handed it to Lei. Lei brought it to numb lips, sipped. "He married that Thai girl you guys rescued from the cruise ship. Anchara."

"No." Lei shook her head. "No. He wouldn't." She sipped again. She couldn't feel anything. Anywhere. Her mind refused to process the words her friend was saying.

Marcella *click-clacked* over to close the door of the office behind Lei, rolling down the blind over the glass window. "I heard it from the Kahului detectives. You remember Gerry Bunuelos, right? Anyway, I had to call over, and he told me this morning. It wasn't recent either—they got married six months ago. Apparently, the woman was going to be deported. Her political asylum application was denied. He told Gerry that he did it to get her a green card, but they've tightened up on that so much the INS has to be convinced it's a real marriage. And they seem convinced."

Lei took another sip of water. Her hand trembled, and the water spilled out onto her shoes, down her slacks. She'd known the chance she was taking when she left for the Academy. She vividly remembered the morning she'd left, when she handed the leash of her beloved Rottweiler, Keiki, to Michael Stevens and got on a plane for Quantico.

She'd struck him a heart-blow that day. It had looked to be a near-mortal one, reflected in the pale granitelike set of his jaw, the arctic blue of his shadowed eyes. He'd accepted the leash she handed him in the parking lot of the airport. Keiki had sat on muscular haunches and leaned her bulk against Stevens's leg. Her triangle ears twitched, worried eyes tracking Lei, sensing Lei's distress. A whimper rumbled in her wide chest.

Lei heard him say the words: "I won't wait for you. I can't wait for you and keep hoping we'll want the same thing."

The same thing. Marriage. Kids.

Lei had heard the words. But that didn't mean she'd believed them. She'd walked away, confident that no matter what he said, he'd wait for her. The hardest thing to leave at that moment had been Keiki, who'd let out an anguished bark as Lei walked into the airport building.

The next thing Lei knew, she was sitting on a hard plastic chair next to Marcella's desk, her head between her knees, Marcella's hand on the back of her neck and her friend's voice in her ear. "Breathe. In. Out. In. Out."

A knock came at the door. "Just a minute!" Marcella snarled. Lei sucked another breath, straightened up.

She'd deal with this later. Much later. Preferably never.

"I'm okay. I just need to get back to work." Lei stood, walked over, and opened the door. Ken Yamada stood there, a crease between his brows.

"What's up?"

"Nothing."

"It's not nothing. Her ex married someone else," Marcella said to Ken.

"I'll be fine. Thanks for the update, Marcella," Lei tossed over her shoulder as she hurried down the shiny hall.

A bright halogen lamp was already on, bathing the workroom table in harsh brilliance. Lei snapped on latex gloves. She took a fresh evidence box out from a folded stack under the table and wrote the newly assigned case number on the label.

Lei took each letter from the stack Max Smiley had given them, carefully unfolded it, and photographed each with its matching envelope and a small numbered tag she set beside the letter so it would show in the photograph.

The room was equipped with two workstations, a long table, a whiteboard against one wall, and a huge window that looked at the ocean—the Federal Building fronted the water on one side. The bulletproof reflective coating on the glass cast a bluish shade to everything in a room already toned in gray.

Ken came in. She glanced up at his frowning face. "Sure you're okay?"

"I will be," Lei said. "I just need to keep working."

"Okay. I'm here if you want to talk about it."

"No thanks." She blinked and blurriness receded; the letter in front of her came clear again. "Thanks for asking, though."

From behind her she could hear the *tappety-tap* of the keyboard as Ken uploaded the photos from the scene and began the ongoing log that would be part of the investigation at every stage. When they had their report well underway, they would e-mail it on the secure internal server to their special agent in charge, Ben Waxman.

Lei watched her hands move through the mechanics of organizing the letters, battening down her pain and racing thoughts, the series of images of Anchara and Stevens together that her mind had begun playing. She had a job to do. She needed to focus on the task at hand. She placed each letter with its envelope on the table and left them spread out. When she had them cataloged, she sat down to read and study them.

"I don't see many postmarks on these," she commented. Most of the letters were typed on cheap computer paper, and most of the envelopes simply read "Smiley" or "Mad Max." A few of them had been mailed to the airline mogul care of general delivery—from nearby areas.

None of the letters were addressed specifically to the estate they'd visited.

"There's a mail slot for each employee at the airline headquarters. Remember what he said? Most of his hate mail came via the suggestion box in the lounge, or in his mail slot. Some were mailed, but he's done a good job of concealing his home address," Ken said.

"Which makes the unsub's ability to find the house even more interesting. Probably narrows the pool of possibilities quite a bit." Lei sorted the letters into different piles: possible threat, simple complaints, definite threat, workplace suggestions. "He doesn't appear to be beloved with the employees."

"Yeah. I see interviewing down at the headquarters as a priority."

"Looks like he's been manipulating people's hours so they don't qualify for health insurance, and he cut health care benefits to the bone." Lei frowned as she made a separate pile for the health care complaints. "We're one of the few states with mandatory health benefits for anyone who works more than twenty hours a week—but Smiley is finding a way around it. You ready to come look at these with me?"

"Almost there. Uploading all the fingerprints from the scene now. I'll start the program scanning for matches, then come take a look."

Lei picked up the Definite Threat pile. "So here are three letters threatening bodily harm to Smiley if they ever get him alone. These aren't signed."

Ken hit a couple more keys, then came to sit on one of the chairs beside her. "Interesting. Even the ones just protesting company policy aren't signed. That tells me no one feels safe speaking up."

"This seems like the kind of workplace that could generate an employee shooting or something."

"I'll see if our NAT at the front office can work up a financial report on the company. Smiley's airline is doing well financially in a tough market. Looks as if he's cut corners in the personnel area. Be right back." Ken left.

A handwritten letter caught her eye.

"You stole from me, and I'm going to find a way to take from you." The letter was signed with a hook-mouthed smiley face.

"I think I found you," Lei whispered as she sprayed the plain lined binder paper with ninhydrin, but nothing fluoresced. Damn. She set the incriminating letter aside and went on to the rest of them.

Ken strode back in with his quick grace. He snapped on a pair of gloves and pulled a rolling stool over. "Greg is working on the employee records. The airline keeps most of that in hard copy though, so he has them photocopying the records for us and they'll be ready for pickup in an hour or so. I was thinking maybe you could pick them up on your way home, get started reading this evening."

"Sounds good." Lei slid the suspicious letter over to him. "Check this out."

"This looks like a real candidate." Ken studied the letter. "You get the prints off this?"

"There weren't any. Got some others, though."

"Okay. I'll get the database looking for a match." He hopped up, got the computer working, and rejoined her at the table. "People are so used to seeing CSI crank out the matches on these things, they don't realize it's usually at least an hour for every set of prints."

He slid a square of matte-finished glass over the paper on the next one they photographed. "Try this when you're shooting from now on. It should help you with the crinkles in the paper."

"Okay." Lei watched him photograph the next one, and together they worked through the remaining stack, uploading the prints and setting the search protocol to go. The desk phone rang and Lei answered it.

"Agent Texeira here." Saying her title still felt a little awkward.

"Agent Texeira, the Paradise Air office called. The employee records are ready for pickup."

"Sounds good. Thanks, Greg." Greg, the NAT, had a nicer phone manner than she remembered having. Lei put the phone down and realized her stomach was rumbling. The digital clock on the wall read 4:00 p.m., and she'd never had lunch. Or breakfast either, come to think of it.

"Done." Ken set down the camera.

"The records are ready for pickup. I think I'll go by and get them, pick up something to eat, and work on reading them at home, like you said."

"Sounds good. I'll call you as soon as we have anything on the prints."

———————

Lei headed down the hall. Through the glass insert in her friend's door, she could see Marcella hunched over her phone at her desk. Spotting Marcella brought back the painful memory of her friend's news. She gave a quick wave, hoping not to have to talk about it again, and headed for the elevator.

"Have a good evening, Agent Texeira." Greg, square-jawed and friendly behind the bulletproof glass, insisted on smiling at her. "I'm making some progress on these online files."

Lei walked back over to him. "Look for a disgruntled employee. We found a letter that seems particularly strong."

"Okay. I'll flag that. Like I told Agent Yamada, they don't have a whole lot of information in the online employee database, but that should be there."

"Thanks." She strode over to the elevator, punched the button.

"You're welcome," the NAT said to her back as she got on, already shrugging out of the crumpled gray linen jacket she wore over a white button-down shirt, Glock in a shoulder holster, and black slacks. The pants were now creased and smeared from the trip to the Smiley estate that morning. Unlike Marcella's band-box perfection, Lei seemed to be a magnet for every spot, stain, and wrinkle, and the formal look of the FBI's dress code was one of the changes in her job that grated on her most.

She hit the Ground button and brushed at the jacket irritably, which did a whole lot of nothing. The doors opened in the dim garage, and she walked to her own vehicle this time, an extended-cab silver Tacoma truck. A brand-new replacement for the Tacoma destroyed on Maui, it had waited for her in storage while she was at the Academy. The vehicle gleamed opal in the dim yellow overhead lights and beeped a greeting, lights flashing, as she hit her Unlock button and climbed in.

Getting in the truck never failed to remind Lei of another thing she'd lost—her Rottweiler, Keiki. The dog usually sat upright beside her on the passenger seat, tongue hanging in a happy doggy grin to be going somewhere, expressive eyes with mobile brown eyebrow patches alight with excitement.

"Oh, Keiki." Lei's chest felt tight with unshed tears as she turned the key, the truck roaring into life. "Damn." She missed her dog so badly.

Not that the hours she put in with the Bureau set her up to be a good dog owner; nor was the apartment she currently lived in the right situation. She navigated the dim garage and got on busy Ala Moana Avenue, heading toward the airport. Paradise Air's business headquarters was among the maze of ancillary buildings beneath the freeway.

Lei bumped along awhile in traffic on the Nimitz Highway, a choked thoroughfare that fed into Pearl Harbor's naval and military installations as well as the airport. Only the arc of brilliant blue sky punctuated with whipped cream clouds showed the beauty of the island—this downtown area could have been any industrial city. Her fingers tapped the wheel impatiently at yet another stoplight.

The tapping of her hand reminded her of when she'd worn Michael Stevens's ring. It had been a pretty, old-fashioned daisy pattern of marquise-cut diamonds until the fire they'd been through on Maui melted it into slag. She reached into her pocket and slipped the disc out, and holding it in her right hand at the top of the steering wheel, turned it in her fingers as she drove the busy highway. As always, she was comforted by the disc's weight, heft, and the roughness of embedded and indestructible diamonds. Michael Stevens had taken the blackened and melted ring to a jeweler. He'd had them clean off the black and hammer it, diamonds and all, into a shape she could carry and rub.

Was that the act of a man who didn't love her? A man who was going to marry someone else only months later?

She found herself squeezing the steering wheel too hard, vision blurred, diamonds in the disc digging painfully into her palm. Her stomach reminded her it was there with a clench of pain, and she spotted a Burger King and pulled off the Nimitz and into the drive-through.

Maybe some food would help.

It didn't take long to buy a couple of burgers and a Diet Coke, get back on the road eating mechanically, and pick up thick folders of personnel records from an aloha-shirted secretary at the Paradise Air building.

Lei pulled into her assigned slot at her apartment building, a forgettable beige cube in the run-down McCully Avenue section of town. The building's only redeeming feature was a huge multicolored shower tree by the entrance that shed pink and yellow petals. Even now, handfuls of petals spiraled down to decorate the hood, misplaced wedding decor.

A bad association, weddings. The food hadn't helped after all—her stomach still hurt. She sucked a deep draft of Diet Coke and got out of the truck, hauling her backpack and the files with her.

No one was around, as usual, and she liked it that way. She climbed the metal stairs on the outside of the building to the third floor, walked down the open walkway with its aluminum baluster to the door of number 314. Sun-faded pistachio, the door looked ordinary enough—but she hadn't sent any misleading messages with jute mats that said Aloha or Welcome.

Lei didn't like visitors. Never had.

She unlocked three different dead bolts with three different keys, and just inside the door, punched in a code to deactivate the alarm. When the dead bolts were back on, she rearmed it and put a bar across the door for good measure. She'd chosen the corner unit so no one could reach her little balcony from any of the other units—the side of the building dropped away to the ground in three stories of blank stucco security. She pulled up a sawed-off broom handle from the track of the sliding door and unlocked it, sliding it open to let in a draft of warm Honolulu evening air, scented from the tree out front.

Lei spread the files out on her low yard-sale coffee table. Even as she opened the top one, she knew she couldn't concentrate—her nerves were too jumpy, her chest still tight with loss and anger—all those jumbled thoughts and images she'd held at bay jostling for attention. She stood and walked to her bare bedroom and stripped the stained and crumpled clothes off a lean, athletic figure, tossing them into the hamper in the corner. She hauled on running shorts, wrestled into an athletic bra, slid socked feet into a new pair of Nikes, and bundled her unruly hair into a ponytail.

A few minutes later she was on the road, headed for downtown Honolulu. As always, she tried to vary her route—but this time her path took her toward another kind of unfinished business.

Chapter 3

*L*ei felt the green-tinted glare off the windows of apartment buildings and storefronts along the avenue. She felt anonymous, shielded by Ray-Ban aviators, curly hair further restrained by a ball cap she'd added and pulled low. She turned up the speed a bit to get her heart rate where she wanted it—and to drown out thoughts of Stevens married. Stevens in bed with the striking Thai woman they'd rescued from human trafficking aboard a cruise ship.

Dark honey skin, wide doe eyes, and a waifish build made Anchara an appealing damsel in distress if there ever was one. Anchara, in danger of deportation back to the home she'd tried to escape, offering Stevens the only currency she had. Stevens, ever the gentleman and rescuer, rebuffed by Lei and lonely...

Lei could see how it had happened, how she'd let it happen. Stevens was a traditionalist at heart. He wanted a family, a white picket fence, someone to cook and greet him with a kiss when he came home from work. Anchara would be thrilled to provide all that, and more.

Probably a lot more.

Lei ran faster, until her breath tore through her lungs in ragged gasps and thoughts of Stevens with Anchara in his arms were pushed out of her mind by the need to concentrate on the sidewalk, passersby that became roadblocks, the inevitable stoplights, which she ignored, racing across the street between cars.

She finally began to tire, slowing to a more reasonable jog, and pulled up in front of a Pepto-Bismol-colored apartment building. Sun-dried magenta bougainvillea tangled in cement planters beside a glass front door whose tinting was peeling.

Lei didn't know what she was looking for. She didn't know why she'd ended up here, but this was Charlie Kwon's old building. She'd come here more than a year ago to confront her childhood rapist, fresh out of jail—and confront him she had.

His murder was still unsolved.

She put her foot up on one of the planters, stretching her hamstrings and tightening her shoelace at the same time.

"Lei Texeira?" A deep male voice.

Lei dropped her foot and spun to face whoever was addressing her. Tall, dark, and handsome didn't do Detective Marcus Kamuela justice—there was something elemental about him. He had a quality of charisma and power that laid-back detective attire of chinos and aloha shirt did nothing to disguise.

"Detective Kamuela! What're you doing down here?" Lei had met Kamuela at a mixer for FBI and Honolulu PD, an attempt by the brass to encourage interagency cooperation. She'd been impressed with what she'd heard of Kamuela's work ethic, not to mention his looks.

"Nothing much. I have an old open murder case here, and I keep hoping something's going to break on it. When I have a little downtime, I come by, observe, see who I can talk to."

"Yeah, I heard you're like a dog with a bone when you get a case." Lei felt her heart thudding with anxiety as well as her hard run. Of all the Honolulu Police Department detectives, Kamuela had to be the one investigating Kwon's murder. She put her other foot up on the planter and tightened that shoelace to hide her betraying face.

"I like to keep a good closure rate." He moved in next to her, leaning on the planter with his hip so he was looking at her. "So you live nearby?"

"Not really. Came down from my place off McCully. I just stopped for a stretch out here. So what case was this?" Might as well see what she could find out.

"Child molester named Charlie Kwon. He hadn't been out of jail ten days before someone popped him in his apartment. What I got on it is too many people with motive and nothing sticking to any of them—there was virtually no physical evidence at the scene. Wish I could let it go; the guy was scum…But he paid his debt, and the parole board swears he was a changed man."

"Stats don't back that up. Child molesters are usually repeat offenders." Lei busied herself with leaning over to place her palms on the warm, rough sidewalk. The feeling of the cement against her palms grounded her. Kamuela didn't have a clue. He had nothing on her, and he didn't know about her abuse, let alone that Kwon was her abuser. "Anyway, nice to run into you."

"Likewise." He smiled a slightly crooked grin with a dimple in one cheek and really white teeth. "And if you hear anything about this Kwon case, let me know." He handed her a card. Her fingers almost wouldn't close over it, but she managed to slip it into her shorts pocket.

"Of course. See ya."

She felt his eyes burning into her back as she jogged up the sidewalk toward her apartment. A platinum-blond woman in a bright pink jean jacket had been spotted at the building the afternoon Kwon was shot and was still wanted for questioning—Lei knew from the news. Marcella had given Lei a pink jacket and platinum wig for fun after the fire—items never seen again in Lei's possessions.

And Marcella had never asked Lei where they were.

Or if she'd shot Kwon.

Marcella might not have noticed the missing items. Lei certainly hoped so. But if she ever needed them, the jacket, rubber gloves, and platinum wig were hiding, gunshot-residue free, in the hollow beam of a storage shed at the police safe house in Kahului.

Just Lei's shit luck that the time her conflicted feet brought her to the building, Marcus Kamuela was waiting outside, a big tiger shark smelling for blood in the water.

The bitch of it was, she hadn't killed Kwon. She'd had him at her feet, all right—the Glock wobbling in her hands as she heard his apology. It hadn't made anything better. If she had shot him she'd at least know what she was up against. As it was, the crime hovered over her life with all the potency of a ticking time bomb.

The answer was obvious.

She needed to somehow solve the case herself. It was the only way she could be sure to be safe—and a part of her really wanted to know who had pulled the trigger.

Lei sped home, barely feeling the miles, she was so preoccupied, and set the detective's card on the edge of the bathroom sink. She stripped out of sweat-soaked running clothes and got into the shower. Half an hour later, turning pruny from hot water, she was ready to get out. She dried off with a threadbare white towel.

Stevens had loved her through broken bones, human bite marks, and terrible bruises. He'd shaved her head when she was injured, his fingers tender on her sensitive scalp. He'd never thought she was anything but beautiful.

Objectively, she knew she looked better than she had many times when they were together. She'd describe herself as a five-foot-six mixed-heritage female of 120 pounds, athletic build, with a taut stomach, small round breasts, and graceful, well-turned arms. Her hair had grown out to touch her shoulders in ringlets that, when orderly, were charming and softened her angular face with its wide, full mouth.

She had nice bones, she concluded, tracing along the length of one collarbone, marked with a jagged scar where a perp had bitten her. But her eyes were her best feature—big, tilted, long-lashed, and a warm brown that changed with her mood.

He'd liked her mouth, too. She remembered how he'd traced her lips with his fingers and gently sucked the pillow of her lower lip into his mouth. She remembered his hands on her breasts, weighing them, flicking and circling her pale tawny-pink nipples with his thumbs until they filled her with a hungry ache. She remembered a necklace of kisses he'd laid across the freckles on her chest.

Yes, she'd been well and truly loved in all the ways a woman could be.

She wrenched her mind away from the memory and walked into the bedroom to dress.

An hour into reviewing the files, Lei found a possible candidate for the burglary—Tom Blackman, age twenty-one, hired for "general duties and baggage handling." Blackman had worked at the airline for six months and used a general delivery mailing address. The file included several write-ups for insubordination, lateness, and one for "calling Mr. Smiley a Nazi and threatening bodily injury against him." A termination notice dated two months ago topped the paperwork in the slim folder.

Lei ran the name in her secure database. Blackman had a sealed juvie record that would take a little doing to open, but no current warrants. She sat back a moment, sipping a glass of water and considering.

Most juveniles who perpetrated a dramatic crime like this had a buildup of antisocial behavior. They'd start with shoplifting and work their way up to jacking a car before they stole a plane. In her mind, the Hawaii unsub was a young white male, angry, with a grudge and a sense of entitlement—and maybe even a sense of humor. Blackman could fit, though she didn't have nearly enough on him yet. Where'd he come from, gone to school? Who were his friends? These things would begin to unlock the puzzle.

Lei was still hungry, her stomach a little upset. She finished the water and set the glass in the sink. Her other few dishes sat lonely in the drainer. She looked in the refrigerator and sighed.

A withered lime and a pair of Coronas still sat in the door of the fridge from when she'd invited Marcella over for a beer they'd ended up being too busy to ever have. On the shelf, a carton of half-and-half, a loaf of wheat bread, and a lump of molding cheddar. In the drawer, an apple and a head of wilting iceberg lettuce.

Lei took the cheddar out, pared off the mold, and ate it with slices of apple. She opened one of the Coronas and slid the glass door open to get more breeze, doing a quick perimeter check below, then sat back down. Her phone buzzed and she picked it up—Marcella was calling.

She just didn't have what it took to talk right now. She let it go to voice mail and then listened: "Hey, Lei. Just calling to see if you're ok, if you want to go out for a drink or something, take your mind off the Stevens thing. Well, text me if you want to. Hang in there, girl."

She texted Marcella back: *Got your message. I'm working and can't go out, but I'm okay. See you tomorrow.*

Luv ya, Marcella texted back.

Having a friend thinking about her was a new thing, and she felt herself warmed, energy renewed by the brief exchange. She spotted another possible—Tyson Rezents, another young male employee at the airline, still employed but often written up for workplace tardiness, caught her eye. No record when she ran him, but he was a senior at nearby McKinley High, where Blackman had also attended. Maybe someone there would know a little more about him.

Other candidates were a Kimo Matthews, twenty-three, fired for stealing from the baggage, and a woman, Lehua Kinoshita, twenty-two, fired for insubordination. Lehua had written a letter protesting getting fired and accusing "Mad Max" of unfair manipulation of her hours to avoid providing her health insurance.

Lei's eyes grew heavy, and she read a few more files before she decided on an early night.

In her bed, a twin-sized blow-up mattress she hadn't bothered to upgrade in two months, she found her eyes wandering around the barren, undecorated room. Lying on that mattress, looking at her clothes in a couple of hampers that passed for the room's furniture, Lei realized she'd never really thought this apartment would be home.

Somewhere in the back of her mind, she'd been getting into a king-sized bed with Michael Stevens, with room at her feet for a big Rottweiler to sleep, in a little plantation cottage on the outskirts of Honolulu. Her lack of furniture, her lack of commitment—they'd been because she didn't know she'd end up alone and dogless.

Lei felt tears well to sting her eyes. Her chest spasmed painfully, and she muffled a soul-deep sob in her pillow. She cried for Keiki, her beloved dog. She cried for Stevens's marriage. She wept out fear, disappointment, loneliness, and sorrow, and finally she slept.

Chapter 4

Morning came too soon, beginning with a bleeding of gray-purple light that welled through the bare window. Lei's sore eyes took in the insultingly cheerful brightening that reflected off the bone-white stucco of the ceiling, filling the room. Her feet felt heavy as lead as she dragged them to the side of the mattress and stood up, straightening the boxers and tank top she'd worn to bed. In the bathroom, her curly hair, still wet when she'd gone to bed, reared up in disarray.

Lei slapped on a squirt of Curl Tamer to deal with it. She changed into another pair of black polyester slacks and another button-down white blouse. She strapped on her shoulder holster, loaded in the Glock, and clipped her shiny new FBI badge onto her waistband.

For the first time, that sense of pride she'd felt touching it wasn't there. She'd traded her Maui Police Department badge for this one—and it was just another cold, hard piece of metal. She'd already been having a hard time adjusting to the FBI, and discovering exactly how much she'd given up for the Bureau wasn't adding to the appeal.

Lei went into the kitchen, opened the fridge. The situation there hadn't changed, and to top it off, she remembered she was out of coffee.

The day was not off to a good start.

At 6:28 a.m., her arms loaded with files, Lei got into her truck. Coffee on the way to McKinley High would have to do. In need of caffeine, she pulled into the nearest Starbucks and did her time in line to get an extra large coffee of the day—Marcella's coffee-drinking ways were wearing off on her. Or maybe that's just what happened in a job like this.

The barista pushed the coffee over to her. "Nice badge."

Lei looked up—he was a surfer dude, sun-streaked blond hair a mass of salty-looking spikes, sea-blue eyes appreciative. Cop fetish, probably—she was alert for those, and immune, at the moment, to male attention.

"Thanks." She took the beverage, walking out without a backward glance.

She called Ken on her Bluetooth as she headed to McKinley High on South King Street, right in the heart of downtown Honolulu. Ken's phone went to voice mail, so she left a message.

"Hey, partner. Following up a lead on a couple of Paradise Air employees at McKinley High School. Call me if anything new breaks."

Lei tapped the Bluetooth at her ear, missing the familiar click of her flip phone as she closed it, the smooth round feel of it as she slid it into her pocket. It had taken her longer than any law enforcement person she knew to switch to a smart phone, and she still missed the sheer physical presence of her old flip phone—like the disc she carried in her pocket, it was something she handled to dispel nerves.

McKinley High was a historic school in the outskirts of Honolulu. Its hundred-year-old administration building had gracefully arched windows and red tile roofing over ivory stucco, a portly bronze of President McKinley holding court at the entrance. Lei walked briskly under great spreading monkeypod trees to the entrance and up worn but immaculate steps to the office.

The staff were prompt and responsive to her badge and no-nonsense demeanor, and revealed that Tyson Rezents had dropped out of school earlier that year.

"He just stopped coming." Principal Tavares was a blocky ex-jock in a polo shirt with a McKinley High logo. "No paperwork filled out."

"Any behavior problems?" Lei asked. "Anything you can tell me about him as a student?"

"No, not really. Poor grades and attendance, the kid works a lot out at Paradise Air. Baggage handler, I understand."

"Okay," Lei said. "This last address—was this with family?"

"I think that's with his mother. They lived together."

"What about Tom Blackman?" The principal confirmed he'd graduated a few years ago, and had nothing to add to that and no current address. Lei headed out, and one of the office ladies touched her arm.

"I knew Tyson. He one good boy, but so much sadness happened to him with his mother. Is he in trouble?"

Lei looked into kind eyes in a round face. The woman's black hair was wound up and pierced by chopsticks decorated with air-dried clay plumerias, a popular local craft.

"No—we jus' like ask him a few questions." Lei let her voice slip into the gentle rhythm of pidgin English, the creole dialect that quickly established trust and belonging among Hawaii residents. The fact that Lei was *from here* and looked the part continued to open doors for her as an investigator.

"Well, I know the principal he wen' give you that old address. But Tyson, he stay living with friends after the mom, she went back to using." The woman drew Lei around the corner of a rack of mailboxes, away from prying eyes.

"Where they stay?" Lei took her spiral notebook out of her pocket.

The woman flipped through a file and produced a card. "Here's his last address with his mother, but I'm not sure if he's still there. He also spends a lot of time with his girlfriend."

Lei's attention sharpened as she looked up from writing down the address. "Do you know where the girlfriend lives, what her name is?"

"She's a student here, that's all. I don't know her name." The woman seemed to have used up her goodwill, and a nervous glance in the direction of the principal's office confirmed this.

"Well, thank you. I may need to call you again."

"I jus' want things to go better fo' that poor boy." The woman shook Lei's hand self-consciously as they said goodbye, and Lei brushed through the waist-high swinging door and out of the administration building.

Lei's cell rang as she climbed into her Tacoma. As always, she checked the caller ID—Ken Yamada was returning her call.

"Hey, partner. Get my message?"

"Yes. Wanted to let you know we've got some employee interviews lined up down at Paradise Air."

"Okay. The boy I came to follow up on, Tyson Rezents, dropped out this year. There's another one, Tom Blackman, and he graduated a couple of years ago. I have two others, young adults fired for stealing and insubordination."

"Sounds worth tracking down. Any of them still working at the airline?"

"Only Rezents. He's the youngest, only seventeen."

"If he's still at the airline, should be pretty easy to interview him there. Bring in those files and we'll focus the interviews a little more, try and get to the ones that really look like they might be connected with the hate letters."

Lei navigated out of the parking lot onto busy South King Street, a quadruple-lane artery that led through the heart of Honolulu. She clicked over to the Bluetooth. "Sounds good." She angled over a few lanes. "So anything back from Waxman?"

Lei was still nervous around the acerbic, immaculate special agent in charge. Marcella had little to say about their boss except a grudging, "He's not bad on a case, but as an administrator, he sucks. He's hard on female agents."

"Waxman looked over the case file so far this morning. Was wondering where you were; said it looked like you ballooned and are coming in late today. Because you phoned me, I was able to fill him in on your activities. Don't do anything without communicating; the Bureau likes all activities to be coordinated."

"You mean, nobody wipes their ass without asking permission," Lei snapped. She still hadn't gotten used to the "teamwork" that went on in the Bureau—she liked to follow hunches and run down her own ideas, and constantly checking in with a chain of command grated. "And what's 'ballooned?' I never ballooned anywhere."

"'Ballooned' is slang for cutting out early, and I'll let that one slide, Texeira." Ken's voice was frosty. "You need an attitude check." He clicked off.

Lei reached in her pocket and took out the white-gold disc, flipping it over as she drove and worked on reining in her irritation. She wondered how Ken could be such an unwavering Bureau poster boy.

But everything was fine. She just had a problem with authority and liked to be independent, and that wasn't something that fit with the culture of the FBI. Those traits were nothing new—they'd even been written in her very first employee evaluation as a lowly patrol officer on the Big Island of Hawaii.

She was just turning into the parking garage at the Federal Building high-rise when her phone rang again. "Texeira."

"Answer the phone with 'Agent Texeira,' please." Ken was still frosty. "And there's been another burglary. Looks like the ultralight flew in, hit the place, and flew out. Meet me at the Acura."

A hit of adrenaline speeded up Lei's reflexes and she pulled the Tacoma in beside the Bureau SUV just as Ken exited the steel garage door from the stairway, his light gray suit jacket unbuttoned and flapping over his weapon and badge. She beeped the Tacoma locked, hopped in the SUV, and they pulled out, lights flashing.

Chapter 5

Sorry for snapping," Lei said, as they turned left out of the garage and headed toward the freeway. "It's hard to get used to all the protocol with the Bureau."

"I get that. But you need to either suck it up or go back to local law enforcement." Ken's stern profile was still turned away from her. "We're the best in the business at what we do. I'm proud to be an agent, and you should be too. It concerns me that, after a year, you're still questioning how we do things."

"Old habits. I just wonder how you are always such a company man about everything when you—you know. Can't be yourself."

Ken's jaw bunched with tension and his eyes narrowed, but he never took his eyes off the road. "I told you. I'm proud to be an agent, and I'm making the necessary sacrifices."

"Okay." Lei knew it was neither the time nor the place for this discussion as they wove through the congested traffic. "I'll keep working on it. So where are we headed?"

"Over the Pali to Kaneohe area again. Big estate butted up against a golf course. I'm guessing the ultralight landed on the golf course and gained access from there."

The cry of the siren and the flashing lights weren't conducive to conversation, especially once they got on the steep and winding Pali Highway and Ken was engaged with driving. Lei concentrated on taming her hair into a bun with bobby pins.

The Pali was a broad artery feeding across the mountains from the Honolulu side of Oahu to the wetter, rainier windward side of the island. Towering mango and albizia trees, swathed in vines, threatened to crowd in over the well-maintained road. Though it was one of the most scenic routes on the island, fast-moving commuters kept it from being a relaxing drive. Sweeping vistas of green drip-castle mountains robed in jungle soared around them, rolling out to a large, shallow bay. Lei was diverted by the views even with the urgency of their speed.

They took a few turns off the highway once on the Kaneohe side, guided by the Acura's refined GPS voice. A pair of huge metal gates decorated with hammered copper flowers and foliage opened wide, leading into the gracious Spanish-style mansion. Lei tried not to be impressed as she stepped out of the SUV, gazing at the arched columns leading in a colonnade from the curved parking turnaround to pair of stained-glass double doors at the front of the house.

A round man with a bald pate and a white Fu Manchu mustache pattered out of the house and up to Lei and Ken. "I'm Silvio Hernandez. The caretaker."

"Eh, Silvio." Ken had a lilt of pidgin in his voice. "What happened here?"

"I always lock up at night; then I go around, open some windows in the house during the day to keep the air moving around. Otherwise the mold, she come bad." Silvio shifted his weight excitedly from foot to foot. "This morning I come around. I walk in the back door; I see one window over the kitchen sink, she stay broke. I go look, and the office, it stay open. The fridge too."

Lei approached the patrol officer near the front door as Ken continued to question the caretaker. "What made your unit think this was our case?"

"Checked with my sergeant this morning. He said call you once he saw this." The uniformed officer led her around the graceful plantings that bordered the house to the seamless melding of green lawn with golf course that rolled away to rugged mountains robed in clouds beyond the course.

A gouged path ending in divots marked the spot where a small aircraft of some type had landed. Farther out, a few chunks of lawn showed where it had taken off again. "The front gates were locked up tight. The caretaker hadn't been turning on the alarm inside the house because he had that routine and really didn't anticipate a burglary from this side."

"Bold move. It does look like it could be related to our case," Lei agreed.

Ken joined them. "Let's take a look inside."

Lei swiveled her head, taking in all the furnishings—classic hacienda-style woven rugs and "rustic" furniture—as Hernandez pointed them down a dark red Mexican-tiled hallway to the back office. The two agents preceded him, hands on their weapons as they checked that the room was clear.

"Dr. Witherspoon and his wife live in the Mainland. Somehow the burglar did this." Hernandez gestured dramatically to the open wall safe, door ajar. "I don't know what they had in there, but it's gone now."

Lei had brought in her crime kit from the Acura and snapped on her gloves. "Any other damage or loss?"

"I think only the kitchen."

"Let's take a look," Ken said. They followed the caretaker into a vast, dim, Mediterranean-looking kitchen done in stone counters and verdigris fixtures. Shining copper-bottomed pots hung from a wrought-iron pot rack in the center.

A hook-mouthed smiley face was scrawled across the silvery surface of the fridge in Sharpie.

"Hm. Familiar unsub." Ken extracted the Canon from its case.

"Can you believe this? And what is 'unsub'?" asked Silvio, hopping from one foot to the other with agitation.

"Unknown subject," Lei said. Ken took his first shot, and the flash reflecting off the refrigerator blinded her. "I'll go look at the safe."

She headed back down to the office, the rubber soles of her black athletic shoes squeaking on the tiled hallway floor. Lei set the crime kit—a matte black aluminum box—on the mission-style desk and popped the metal hasps.

Nested in the foam interior were packets of evidence swabs, swatches of peel-off fingerprint retrieval tape, a wide, soft powder brush, spray bottles of luminol and ninhydrin, a measuring tape, a digital camera, and several screw-top canisters of fingerprint powder. She even had a roll of expensive gelatin tape for the new fingerprint technology.

Opening and looking through the well-stocked case always gave her a warm, contented feeling—she wondered if that was how other women felt looking at a closetful of clothes.

She removed the camera first and took pictures of the office from various angles. Nothing appeared out of place but the partway-open safe and a cowboy painting leaning on the wall beside it.

Lei photographed the medium-sized, wall-mounted safe. It had a dial mechanism with a shiny chrome handle, and the interior, lined with a single shelf, was empty. She pushed the door a little wider, and this time she saw the familiar hook-mouthed smiley face scrawled on the interior of the door.

"I wonder what that's about," she muttered, as she took a few more shots of it. "Is it still about Max Smiley, or is it some kind of personal statement?"

She unscrewed one of the fingerprint-powder canisters (she chose white, to contrast with the matte black surface of the safe), swirled the brush in the powder, and applied it to the safe in gentle spinning motions. The long, soft nylon bristles splayed the powder generously over the surface. She pumped a couple of gentle puffs of air from a rubber bulb over the door, including the metal handle.

"Anything?" Ken's voice from behind her made her jump.

Lei carefully applied one more puff of air. All of the white powder drifted away and decorated the floor beneath the safe.

"Doesn't look like anything on the outside." She prodded the safe open with a gloved finger. "Check out the smiley face in here. He's thumbing his nose at somebody."

"Attitude is a part of this for sure. I didn't find any prints on the fridge or cabinets."

"I'm still pretty stumped on how the unsub got the safe open." Lei turned back, spun the powder over the surface of the desk. Puffs from the bulb brought up prints, but the knob used to pull the desk drawer was clean. Lei tugged the drawer open—and a three-by-five card greeted her. She picked it up by the edges. On the back, in faded ballpoint pen, a series of numbers were printed.

"Apparently, this was lying around somewhere. All the unsub had to do was find it."

Silvio Hernandez trotted up, holding up a cell phone. "Dr. Witherspoon wants to talk to you." Ken took the phone as Lei went back to fingerprinting the interior of the safe.

"Special Agent Yamada here."

From where she was dusting, Lei could hear indignant squawks from the phone.

"I understand you're upset, Dr. Witherspoon. We are just beginning our investigation, and it would help us greatly to know what you had in your safe." Ken was unflappable, as usual.

More squawking.

"Yes, I'm afraid so. The safe was wide open. We found a card in your desk with the combination on it. So did the thief. Why don't you fax an inventory of what was in the safe to our office?" Ken walked slowly around the room. Lei knew he was looking for anything that might have been dropped or lost by the burglar. He wrapped up the phone call with the homeowner, making soothing noises about insurance claims and speedy recovery.

Ken definitely had a way with people, and Lei knew there was a lot about that she could learn from him. Each of her partners—first in the police department, now in the FBI—had had something to teach her. She finished up the safe, shook her head.

"Nothing. It was wiped, because there's nothing left behind by Witherspoon either."

"Same in the kitchen." Ken handed the phone back to Hernandez. "Your boss said he has a fax machine here and he's having the inventory of the safe faxed to that number. Do you know where it is?"

"Follow me." Hernandez hurried off, with Ken close behind.

Lei packed up her supplies and carried the case into the kitchen, where a visual survey revealed a similar snowfall of fingerprint powder and not a whole lot else. She opened the towering Sub-Zero refrigerator and looked inside.

Hernandez returned. "Dr. Witherspoon, he like me keep some supplies on hand for if they return unexpected. Cheese, eggs, bread, some lunch meat and fruit..."

Lei pulled out the interior drawer. "Nothing in here at all."

"Yeah, that's what I told the other agent—he cleaned out the fridge."

Ken returned, carrying a couple of faxed sheets. "Quite a haul here. Mr. Hernandez, can you step out a moment and give us some privacy?"

Hernandez's white brows twitched and he huffed out, offense

in every stiff line of his body. Ken looked at Lei, his straight dark brows drawn together with concern.

"There were at least ten thousand dollars in that safe and a good deal of jewelry. There was a loaded gun in there, too. Walther PPK."

"The gun of the James Bond fan. That raises the stakes." Lei felt her heart sink for the burglar with an attitude who'd stolen a Chihuahua and left behind smiley faces. Her intuition was still telling her this wasn't an adult—but they had little to go on in developing a profile.

"Yeah. We have to be prepared to use deadly force now." Ken didn't look any happier than Lei felt. "Let's get on the road. We still have interviews down at Paradise Air."

Chapter 6

*L*ei pushed at ringlets springing free from the bobby-pinned bun she'd corralled them into, using the mirror over the sink of Paradise Air's employee restroom. A shadow moved behind her, and a hefty-built woman in a Paradise-Air-logo-covered aloha shirt moved in behind her.

"You the FBI agent here to talk to us?"

Lei turned, extended her hand. "Yes, one of them. Special Agent Lei Texeira."

"Reynalda Tamayose." The woman waved a little in lieu of shaking. "I came in to wash."

"Sure." Lei moved aside so Reynalda could wash her hands. "Yes, we're investigating the theft of a small aircraft from Max Smiley's house."

"Probably that little silver toy Hummel of his." Reynalda made a face at herself in the mirror, checking her teeth. They were unnaturally white. The woman's face had the immobility of Botox and the patina of a good deal of makeup. "I'm one of the personnel managers. Been with the company since it was just Max and his first couple of pilots back in the early eighties."

"We were wondering about some of the workplace policies, especially around health care and vacation. According to some of the correspondence Mr. Smiley gave us, employees weren't happy with the conditions."

"Mr. Smiley going to get to see the notes from the interview?"

"Of course not. Everything to do with the investigation is confidential."

"Then I've got a few things to say." Reynalda led the way out of the restroom. "I'd like to be interviewed first."

Lei followed her to the conference room they'd been assigned for the interviews. It didn't look like it had been updated since the company began in the eighties: mint-green wall-to-wall, flattened by the tracks of chairs, was leavened by a Pegge Hopper print in faded pastel tones on one wall.

Ken Yamada was setting up a small video camera on a tripod as they entered. Lei made introductions. "Special Agent Yamada, this is Reynalda Tamayose, one of the personnel managers."

"Welcome, Reynalda. Thanks so much for helping out with the investigation." The smile Ken gave Reynalda was so brilliant, so warm, Lei saw the older woman get melty in the knees as she sank into one of the molded plastic chairs.

"Of course. Anything I can do."

Lei signaled him to turn on the equipment, and as he did so, Lei stated the woman's name, the date and time, and hurried on, eager to ride the wave of disclosure begun in the restroom.

"So, Reynalda. You've been with the company how long?"

"Thirty years. Since the beginning." Lei saw the woman sneak a once-over at Ken.

"And you've known Max Smiley all that time?"

"Yes."

"What kind of employer would you say he is?"

"He's good to those who don't complain, who show up to

work every day, and who are willing to suck it up to keep a job. I've been one of them."

"So it seems like it's been a tough place to work in some ways." Ken let his statement trail off encouragingly.

"Well." Reynalda batted her eyes at him. "I've done well here. I started as a baggage handler and receptionist. Now I'm one of two managers."

"So you must be an exemplary employee."

"Max seems to think so."

"So does he give you a lot of responsibility for the day-to-day operations?" Lei asked.

"Yes. I do the scheduling of employees, a lot of the hiring and firing."

"So what can you tell us about who might have had an ax to grind with Max Smiley?" Lei noticed Reynalda had turned away from her, angling her body toward Ken. She raised an eyebrow at her partner, and as smoothly as passing a baton in a race, he picked up the thread.

"Yes, Reynalda. You seem to have been in a unique position to monitor and implement Max's policies."

"I had a part to play, sure. But I didn't make the rules. Max told me to schedule people nineteen hours a week every month so they didn't qualify for health insurance—so I did. Didn't mean I liked doing it. When they came in to complain, I told them what I'm telling you. I just followed orders, or my head was next." Reynalda took a packet of Virginia Slims out of her pocket, tapped them on the table. "Mind if I smoke? It's against regulations, but I'm the boss in this office, and I'm not gonna tell."

"Of course not," Ken said smoothly, but Lei saw by the flare of his nostrils that he did mind. She got up and turned on an overhead fan and cracked the door as Reynalda produced an empty Diet Coke can from her pocket and lit her cigarette. Ken looked through the stack of employee files in front of him, pulling out the four possibles Lei had flagged as they waited for Reynalda to complete her first deep drag on the cigarette.

"We've had to let a lot of people go over the years," Reynalda said. "One of the worst ones recently was a young guy named Tom Blackman." Reynalda's arched brows drew together, her painted-on mouth puckering hard as she took a pull on her cigarette. "Sassy little punk."

"Sounds like he had an attitude problem." Ken had Blackman's folder open, leafing through the slim paperwork.

"He had a few friends, but no one goes against Max when he makes a decision to fire someone." Lei noticed the transition from "Mr. Smiley" to "Max" as the woman got more comfortable. "Yeah. He's a guy with an ax to grind with Max. Kid had some piercings; Max told him to take them out—he was old-fashioned that way. Tom was on the baggage handling line; he didn't think it mattered and told Max so. They had words. Max fired Tom."

"Anything else about this young man stand out?" Ken asked.

"He was late pretty often. We also thought he was stealing from the baggage, but we never caught him at it. Insubordination was a good excuse to fire him."

Lei made a couple of hash marks next to Tom Blackman's name.

"So, what can you tell us about a kid named Tyson Rezents?" Ken transitioned smoothly to the suspect whose age and history made him Lei's next-favorite suspect.

"Good kid. Been loading bags here part-time since he was fifteen, and he's seventeen now. He's had a tough life—mom's a crack whore. The company is kind of a family to him."

"Tell us more."

Reynalda tapped ash off her cigarette into the can. "I'm wondering how long this is going to take."

Ken reengaged her with a smile and a nod. "Just a couple

more questions—you've been so helpful. Has Rezents ever expressed any unhappiness with the company, or with Max Smiley specifically?"

"Not that I know of. Max put the suggestion box in the lounge mainly so he can keep track of what people are saying and let them think he gives a shit about morale, which he doesn't."

"Where can we find Rezents?"

"I don't know if he's on today. He checks in over at the airport. I only see him when he's picking up a check or something."

"We want to know about a few more people, but can you find out if Rezents is working when we're done? I know this is an imposition—we so appreciate your time," Ken said.

"What else do you want to know? I'm all yours."

Lei managed to keep a straight face by looking back down at her list of names as the older woman slanted a thick-mascaraed glance at Ken.

"We had a couple more employees who'd been fired. Lehua Kinoshita and Kimo Matthews."

Reynalda tipped her head, exhaled smoke from her nostrils. "More punks. We've definitely had a few over the years. Lehua was going on and on about the health insurance, so we just told her she'd be happier elsewhere. She tried to turn us in to the Department of Consumer Affairs, but I was able to show legitimate work patterns that justified her scheduling when the inspector came. Kimo, he stole from the bags." She tapped her ash. "Passengers filed missing items claims and HPD found the items at a local pawnshop and Kimo on camera. So we fired him."

"Either of them express any particular hostility?" Ken asked. His dark eyes were narrowed against the smoke.

"Kimo knew he'd been fairly busted. He was happy to just get his last check and take off. But Lehua said she wasn't going to give up. She'd made a list of employees whose hours had been manipulated or who'd had health care unfairly denied."

"Do you have a list of those names?" Lei asked, keeping her excitement under control.

"Yeah. I told her all sweetlike that I wanted to look into it, talk Max into making it right for these people, and she gave it to me."

Lei looked up from her note-taking at Reynalda's smug face. This woman wasn't just taking orders—she was enjoying her job of being Max Smiley's enforcer. Ken, on Reynalda's other side, must have seen Lei's face, because he frowned, giving her a tiny head shake.

"We'd sure appreciate a copy of that." Lei smiled with difficulty. So far her sympathies were squarely with the employees.

Reynalda stubbed out her cigarette, tucked the pack into the front pocket on her shirt, and picked up the can. "Follow me."

They trailed her to a small, tidy cubicle. Reynalda threw the Diet Coke can into the trash, went to her computer, and punched up a few keys. "I'll print Rezents's schedule for you, as well." A minute later, the schedule and a typed list popped out of the printer. She picked the schedule up, frowned as she looked at it. "Tyson was supposed to be on yesterday. Never showed up."

"Does he make a habit of that?" Lei asked.

"Remember I told you about Max's criteria for a good employee? Showing up is number one. So no. We write people up and fire them after two no-shows."

"Can we get his contact information?" Ken asked.

"Aren't I supposed to have a warrant or something?" Reynalda batted her eyes at him.

"Mr. Smiley seemed to want us to have the company's full cooperation. I'm sure it's fine, but you're welcome to call him and check." Ken smiled back at her.

"No, that's all right." She punched a few more buttons and they waited for the whir of the printer; then she handed over a copy of Tyson Rezents's contact information.

"Thank you. You've been amazing." Lei was already opening the door to leave as Ken doled out his final flirtation.

"No problem. Call me if you need anything else," Reynalda said. "Anytime."

Lei looked at the new address and compared it with the one she had from the high school. "I'm guessing he's not with his mother anymore."

Ken plugged the kid's more recent address into the Acura's GPS, pulled out of the parking lot and back onto busy Nimitz. Lei booted up the Toughbook computer from a modified compartment in the dash. Her fingers flew over the keys as she inputted Rezents's social security number and birthdate into the database. A couple of minutes later, the boy's profile popped up.

"Rezents has a couple of misdemeanors. Drunk and disorderly, a *pakalolo* possession charge."

"Any of them look good for this, then." Ken's gaze focused on driving as they wound into the older, run-down McCully Avenue neighborhood where Tyson lived.

"Except maybe Kimo Matthews—seems like he wasn't mad at Paradise Air, though he's a proven thief." She punched up Kimo's record. "Looks like he's got a warrant out; didn't show for his court date on the baggage robbery charges."

"Hm." Ken was thoughtful, his eyes narrowed. "So what are you thinking?"

"I'm thinking about family history—with Rezents starting work so early, I wonder if he's got a chip on his shoulder, maybe because of this druggie mom of his. Decides to stick it to the man in a way that will be remembered."

"That works for me, too."

"Speaking of working—you worked Reynalda pretty well."

"Like you said—the gaydar misses me when it needs to."

"I'm not judging. I meant it as a compliment—you do interviewing really well."

Ken grinned. "I have my ways."

"Now that that other place was hit, don't you think we should consider whether this is even related directly to Paradise Air and Max Smiley?" Lei asked.

"I've been wondering about that, too, but until we have further leads, we need to keep going in this direction."

"Okay." Lei kept digging, using one of the programs the FBI used to track online activity. "Rezents has an online presence. Pops up in chat rooms on the Occupy movement. He's also got a Facebook page." She scrolled through his timeline. "Lots of angry rants about the one percent. I'm liking him more for this every minute."

"Any family connections that you can find?"

"Wait a minute." She went back to the tax database, pulled up parents' names. "No father on his birth certificate. His mother is Shawna Rezents—and boy does she have a record. Prostitution, petty theft, and several counts of child abuse. This kid's had it rough."

They pulled up in front of a sun-blasted beige duplex under a tired monkeypod tree in a neighborhood not far from Lei's. Lei got out, looking for the mid-1990's white Ford Ranger registered to Tyson Rezents—a vehicle so ubiquitous to Hawaii it might as well be a Toyota Tacoma.

"His truck's gone," Lei said as they walked up a short cement path to the front door. "Doubt he's here."

Ken didn't answer, just knocked—three hard raps.

Nothing.

Ken's hand was raised for another knock and Lei's rested instinctively on her weapon as the door opened abruptly.

A girl hung in the doorframe, blinking at the invasion of sun and law enforcement. Raccoon shadows of old makeup ringed her eyes, and loose breasts fought for freedom in a thin tank top.

"Yes?" Voice like rattling gravel in a coffee can.

"We're looking for Tyson Rezents," Lei said.

"He's not here. He's at work."

"He's not at work; we checked. Are you his girlfriend?"

"No. Roommate." Another shadow crowded from behind—a looming male one. "We share the place with Tyson. What's going on?"

"Nothing. We just want to ask him a few questions." Lei didn't want to tip their hand that the FBI was looking for Rezents if they could help it. She tried a friendly smile—which didn't seem to be working because the boyfriend moved up into view, meaty hand on the girl's shoulder, unshaven jaw resting on her bed-snarled head.

"Who are you?" he growled.

"We'll be back," Ken said. They withdrew, leaving the cave-dwelling couple staring at the Acura as they pulled away. "I like it that I didn't have to tell you it's too early for Rezents to know we're looking for him."

"You forget I came up from patrol officer to detective before I joined the Bureau," Lei said. "Lots of times we wanted to ask a few questions without someone knowing we were cops."

"Well, I'm sure they made us for cops, but they don't have to know what kind. That's one thing about the Bureau—once people know they're being investigated, they get scared, and word spreads fast."

"I can see that." Lei programmed the address Reynalda had given them for Tom Blackman into the GPS. "Maybe Black-man's home."

Another run-down neighborhood, this time a little cinder-block cottage with "ornamental" holes in the cement brick lining the walkway. A faded plastic play set occupied a scrap of dandelion-choked front yard.

"Yes?" A petite woman in a muumuu stood behind a steel-screened door.

Ken took the lead. "Hi. Do you know a Tom Blackman?"

"Yes."

"Is he home?"

"Doesn't live here anymore."

"Do you know where he went?"

"I kicked him out. He hadn't paid his rent. And no, he didn't leave an address."

Lei consulted her notes as Ken fired up the Acura. "Let's go look for Lehua Kinoshita now—we shouldn't focus in on these two too early. Let's call in that warrant on Kimo Matthews, step up finding him," Ken said. Lei got on the phone to Dispatch and had them call in to HPD that Matthews was now wanted for FBI questioning.

"I'm looking for info on Lehua," Lei said, working the Tough-book.

"She seems like a straight shooter. She was trying to get jus-tice for herself and others at Paradise. Do you think that fits with a vandalizing burglar?" Ken asked.

"Not sure, but I agree we shouldn't zero in on anyone too early." Lei had Lehua's profile up. "No criminal activity, not even a parking ticket. She's clean."

"Doesn't mean she didn't have an ax to grind with Smiley, though. Do you have an address?"

"Yes." Lei plugged it into the GPS. "Next stop, health insur-ance activist. I think we should also check how far the range is on the Hummel. Maybe we can figure out where the unsub is going next." Lei worked the Toughbook as Ken negotiated clogged traffic back into downtown. "Whoa. Looks like the Hummel can do up to a hundred twenty-five miles on a tank of gas. That's range enough to get to another island."

Chapter 7

Suppressed urgency infused the office upon their return—they'd received an abrupt summons back to the Bureau as they left the unoccupied apartment that was Lehua Kinoshita's last-known address.

Special Agent in Charge Waxman sat at the head of the shiny fake-burled-wood conference table. Waxman, pale as his name suggested, with a silver comb-over and a dapper suit, opened up a laptop. Special Agent Gundersohn, a large and deceptively slow-moving Swede, sat at Waxman's right hand. On his other side, Marcella and her partner, Matt Rogers, had taken seats. Lei and Ken took a few more chairs to cluster at one end of the lengthy table.

The conference room was a strictly utilitarian space, sound-proofed walls lined in whiteboard and a single large plaque with the FBI logo on it behind Waxman's head. A heavily tinted bullet-proof glass window looked out on a wind-whipped cobalt ocean dotted with fishing and sailboats. "Lei and I were just coming back from the field to brief you as to where we are on the case." Ken let his statement turn into a question as Sophie Ang, specialist from the IT department, slipped into the chair beside him, already opening her own laptop.

"Yes, and I want to hear it—but first you're going to want to see this." Waxman pushed a button on the bottom of the table and a projection screen whirred down behind his head. Another button and the webpage on his laptop leaped into view. SMILEY BANDIT REDISTRIBUTES WEALTH was the title of a plain white blog page. Lei's heart jumped. The unsub was making some sort of move.

A grainy photo showed a picture of the front of the Institute for Human Services, Honolulu's biggest homeless shelter. A small cardboard box sat on the cement steps leading up to the shelter.

Waxman clicked to the next photo. The picture was of the interior of the box. It was filled with a mound of jewelry and stacks of rubber-banded cash.

"*A donation was made to Institute of Human Services in the name of Dr. Nathaniel Witherspoon, part-time Hawaii resident and full-time member of the one percent,*" was the caption.

Ang's long tawny fingers worked her keyboard like braille, her triangular face intent. She was a tall, fit-looking mixed-race black woman Marcella had introduced as a friend, but Lei didn't know her well yet. "Trying to get an IP on that blog address."

"Whoa. This some kind of Robin Hood gig?" Matt Rogers was from Texas and hadn't bothered to blend—he wore a blond military cut, extra set of muscles, and boots under his chinos.

"It's beginning to look that way," Waxman said. "This blog link was sent to all the major news networks, and the phones have been ringing off the hook—and we've got a whole lot of nothing to say at the moment. We had the shelter put the box somewhere safe so we can pick it up and check it for evidence. In the meantime, I'm bringing Scott and Rogers in on the case for extra support."

Waxman hit another button, and the overhead screen filled

with a bright silver aircraft—all graceful, rounded lines. It was hard to believe Max Smiley had assembled it from a kit.

"We had a chance to run a little research. Unlike many ultralights, the Hummel's more like a real airplane. It has a max speed of eighty miles an hour and a range of one hundred twenty-five miles," Ang said.

"We were just looking into that, too. A hundred twenty-five miles is far enough to fly to Maui," Lei said. "He could escape Oahu."

"It would be very dangerous," Gundersohn said. "There are strong winds; it's all ocean to cross."

"And the maximum height the plane can go is ten thousand feet." Ang's eyes were still on her screen as her fingers flew. "I'm not getting anything useful off this blog post."

"This is probably a kid. He might not realize what he's taking on. He might not know how dangerous it is." Lei pictured the tiny craft bucking its way across that long hundred miles.

Ang was still working her keyboard but took a second to look up at Lei through the black bangs of a pixie cut. "What makes you think it's a kid? You sound sympathetic."

"I don't know for sure that it's a kid, but I think so. We haven't had time to fill you in on all we've pulled together on the unsub." Lei produced her spiral notebook, earning an amused glance from Marcella, who was always after her to switch to using her smartphone. "We have four possibles with motive and negative history with Max Smiley and Paradise. They're aged seventeen to early twenties, and Ken and I think the attitude, the graffiti, and the theft of the dog point to someone young and at least a little impulsive."

"Agent Scott, take notes for us please," Waxman said. Lei spotted Marcella's tiny eye roll; Marcella's theory about why he always picked her to take notes was that the SAC liked her ass to provide visual entertainment for meetings.

They all looked at Marcella's rounded behind as she turned her back to the group, picked up a marker, and uncapped it. She reached high to write TOM BLACKMAN, TYSON REZENTS, KIMO MATTHEWS, and LEHUA KINOSHITA on the boards as Lei read the names off to her, jotting down details under each as Lei and Ken elaborated.

Lei didn't see the appeal—Marcella's ass was round and high, but a little big, in Lei's opinion. Why just look at that, when one of her friend's top buttons had come undone, hinting at some truly stunning cleavage? Lei felt a pang of envy—it was hard to look at any part of Marcella without staring.

"So what else?" Marcella asked, gesturing with the pen.

"We think Blackman has the strongest motive," Ken said. "He's got a record, he has an attitude, and he was fired for threats against Smiley. Haven't found him yet, though—he doesn't appear to have an address. Kimo Matthews already has an arrest warrant out, and we bumped that to a priority BOLO."

Marcella jotted the information. Her white shirt rode up and exposed a patch of golden skin at her tiny waist. Maybe Marcella's butt wasn't really that big—it just seemed that way contrasted with her small waist and those full breasts. This was not a problem Lei would ever have, with her slim hips and B-cup bra size.

Lei bit the inside of her cheek. She'd never worried about her attractiveness, hardly noticing herself in the context of other women before—she'd been too busy surviving. Since when did she care that other women were prettier?

Maybe since her ex married a gorgeous Thai girl.

Lei's mind provided a mental picture of Anchara's tiny, round butt with that long black hair swishing over it, so long it touched the backs of her thighs. Lei pinched herself viciously through her pants to stop the mental torture, and her hand crept into her pocket to rub the white-gold disc—but that only reminded her of her loss.

She yanked her hand out of her pocket. *Focus on the case, Texeira!* "Tyson Rezents is only seventeen years old. Until this morning, when he didn't show up for work, he was an employee of Paradise Air." Lei filled them in on the connections they'd made on Rezents so far.

Ken gestured to Lei. "Tell the group why you think he's good for this." He was giving her an opportunity in front of the group to expand on the ideas she'd been working.

"Rezents has had a rough deal. Mom's a druggie and a prostitute. He's been in and out of foster care, and he's got a chip on his shoulder about the wealthy. I saw a Facebook page with a lot of rants about the 'one percent,' and I notice that's in the blog caption."

"Here it is." Ang had been busy. Her screen popped up next to Waxman's. Rezents's Facebook page looked like it had been edited. She didn't see the political cartoons she'd spotted before, and the rhetoric had been purged.

"That's not what it looked like when I first saw it," Lei said.

"Agent Ang, spend some time on each of these suspects, work up some in-depth background. Also, see if you can put some kind of trace on that website, see where it came from and when our unsub uploads to it. Scott and Rogers, you're on Tom Blackman. Texeira and Yamada, you're on Rezents, since you already have some traction there. And, Texeira, you have some law enforcement connections on Maui—alert them. Let's do an all-islands priority BOLO in case he makes a run for it." Waxman retracted the overhead screen, signaling the meeting was over.

Lei gathered her coffee mug and notes. Her heart began a slow thud. She had a reason to call over to Maui, whether she wanted to or not. And she might end up speaking to Stevens when she did.

Chapter 8

Lei punched the numbers on the phone decisively.

"Haiku Station."

"Lieutenant Omura, please."

"Just a moment." A slack-key guitar rendition of Muzak filled her ear while the call was transferred to her former commanding officer at Haiku Station on Maui. Lieutenant Omura was a formidable woman—one Lei was still intimidated by—but in the course of an investigation last year, she had come to respect her.

"Omura here."

"This is Special Agent Lei Texeira calling from Oahu."

"Lei! Excellent, I heard you graduated. How are you?"

"Fine. Thanks, Lieutenant."

"Captain, thank you very much. I'm in the middle of moving my office to Kahului Station. Captain Corpuz took early retirement, and I'm taking his place."

"Congratulations! Even better that I got ahold of you today. This is an official call." Lei filled Omura in on the investigation and the possibility of the ultralight's flight to Maui. "We think it's a kid. He's hit two big houses here and is pissing off some very important people, and if he makes it to Maui, it's going to be by the skin of his teeth."

"You should alert the Coast Guard, too," Omura said. Lei could tell she was taking notes. Lei experienced the bladder cramp her former commander could still engender at the reminder of something Lei wished she'd thought of. "Yes, we already did that." Lei mentally crossed her fingers and hoped Waxman had taken care of it.

"We got the fax on this BOLO, but I'll cover it in this morning's all-island briefing—put our people on high alert. Now, there's someone here who I know would like to say hi."

Lei felt the blood drain from her face at the possibility of speaking to Stevens, but it was Pono's rumbling bass that came over the line.

"Sweets!" Her former partner was never going to stop calling her that misnomer of a nickname, inspired by the Bing Crosby song "Sweet Leilani."

"Pono Kaihale. It's been a while." She looked down at the yellow legal pad on her desk, drawing circles and blinking back tears. Pono had been like a big brother. She'd missed him more than she'd let herself realize. "When are you and Tiare coming over here?"

He snorted. "You know what we make. The kids are in school at Kamehameha now. We don't take trips anywhere but to soccer games."

"Shoots. I was just thinking about you guys. How's everything?"

"Same smell. Iceheads, potheads, tourists getting robbed— just another day in paradise. Let me call you later. I'm sure the captain needs her phone. Still got the same number?"

"No." Lei gave him her new cell phone number. "Talk to you later."

She hung up and realized she'd drawn hearts, with her name

in them, all over the page. They were all variations on the tattoo Stevens had had done when they were on Kaua`i—a tiny purple heart with LEI in it, inside his forearm near the crook of his elbow.

She wondered if he'd had it lasered off yet.

This was why she didn't contact her old friends. They all reminded her of what she'd left behind and lost.

"Sounds like the Maui people are on it," Ken said from his desk. She'd been so absorbed, she'd forgotten he was in the room.

"Yeah. They got our fax, but my old commanding officer is going to highlight it on the all-island daily alert. She reminded us about notifying the Coast Guard, too. She's been promoted to captain of Kahului Station."

"Yeah, Coast Guard got the BOLO too. Nice to talk to old friends?"

"A little mixed. I miss them. Some of them, at least. Okay, what next?"

"Let's go out and pick up that box from the homeless shelter. See if there's any new trace on it. It's time to step things up."

Ken pulled the Acura up in front of the Institute for Human Resources, right in the red zone in front, as Lei snapped off the siren/lights—time was of the essence now, and with the lights on, getting through downtown traffic hadn't been the usual hassle.

They hurried up the cement steps, passing several homeless sitting in the sun. Lei glanced at their umbrellas and shopping carts, realizing her attitude had changed from annoyance to sympathy in the years she'd been a cop—homeless in Hawaii was warmer than other places, but still no picnic in the park, and the reasons that led to it were never simple.

They walked into the urban-ugly building and down the hall to a receptionist. Lei had her cred wallet out first. "Special Agents

Texeira and Yamada. We are here to pick up the box left on the front steps."

"It's in the director's office." The girl hustled out from behind the desk, led them down the hall, and knocked on another door.

"Come in!"

Ken and Lei showed their creds again to the short, balding man behind a battered aluminum desk. "Tell us about the box," Ken said.

The director moved the box over in front of them, holding it gingerly with a pair of tissues. "I'm sorry. Our receptionist touched it when she brought it in. Kind of remarkable when you think about it, that no one took it."

"Why would they?" Lei said as they looked at the box—a nondescript square. Ken snapped on rubber gloves, picked it up, lifting the flaps to look inside at the contents—bundled cash and jewelry matching the description of what had gone missing in the most recent hit.

"Lei, can you get the receptionist's fingerprints, so we can rule them out?"

"Sure—but just a minute." She reached inside her jacket for the driver's license photos of Rezents, Kinoshita, Blackman, and Matthews, slid them across the desk to the director. "Seen any of these people?"

"Yes." The director tapped the photo of Blackman. "He's been our guest recently."

"Is he still here?"

"No. Checked out last week, said he had a line on a place."

"Any idea where that is?"

"Check with the receptionist. She has the clients fill out an exit form. Maybe he left some information on that."

"Anything you can tell us about him?"

"Angry young man. Our social worker tried to counsel him, but he refused. Seems like he thinks the world owes him something."

Ken scooped up the box, and the director peered at him over his reading glasses. "We're going to ask for that donation to be honored."

"That's your business," Ken said. "We will return it to the owner when we're done using it for evidence, and what he does from there is between you."

Lei hurried back down the hall to the receptionist. "I need your prints to rule you out on the box and any information you have on Tom Blackman."

"Oh, Tom?" The receptionist seemed to perk up, and Lei noticed she was an attractive young brunette with a skull tattoo on her breast bobbing distractingly in and out of her neckline. "Is he in trouble?"

"No. We just heard he might have information related to a case we're working on." Lei opened her box for the fingerprint kit. She rolled the girl's fingers across the pad and onto a card. "Do you know where he went after he checked out?"

"I have the exit form." They finished the fingerprinting and Lei handed her a wipe. She rubbed her hands and opened a file cabinet, took out a bulging file. "We don't do a lot of paperwork here, just an intake and exit form basically. He didn't leave an address." She pointed with a purple-tipped nail at the empty line.

"Did Tom tell you anything?" Ken had joined Lei.

"Yeah, he said he had a place with a friend from the airline. Said it was going to be a little crowded, but just until he got on his feet and got another job."

Out at the car, Lei looked at Ken. "I know we need to take the box back in and check it over, but do you think it's worth another drive out to Rezents's place? I mean, those guys are around the same age."

"I was actually thinking we should look for Rezents's mother's last-known address. Blackman isn't from here, but Rezents is. Maybe the mother will know something."

"Good idea." Lei punched up Shawna Rezents on the Tough-book. "Got something here. She's not far away, if this address is still good."

Ten minutes later, Ken pulled the Acura into a potholed driveway in front of yet another sun-blasted apartment building, narrowly missing a blond woman running out the door. The face Lei saw flash by the window was the once-pretty, hard-used kind.

A portly man pursued her, and Lei opened her door, blocking him. "Can I help you?" she asked, stepping into his way as Ken bolted after the woman in the driver's license photo they'd just been perusing.

"She owes me rent!" the man yelled. "Stop her!"

Ken had a hand on the woman's arm, and as Lei and the land-lord watched, they spoke. Then he took his hand off, releasing her, and she broke into a jog, moving rapidly away.

"Stop her, goddamn it!" the landlord yelled, face reddening, as Ken returned, smoothing his immaculate jacket.

"Not our problem." He cocked his head at Lei. The two agents got into the Acura.

"What kind of cops are you?" the landlord yelled after them as they pulled out. "I'm filing a complaint!"

"That's what I don't miss about local law enforcement." Lei rolled up her tinted, bulletproof window so she didn't hear the invectives spewing after them as they drove away. "Does she know anything about Tyson?"

"She says she hasn't seen him in months. She was pretty eager to get away; I think she was telling the truth."

"So he's in the wind," Lei said. "Interesting. They all are."

Chapter 9

Lei had a simple system for her clothes: dirty clothes all in one plastic hamper. Take to basement. Separate by colors. Work clothes came out of the dryer and went straight onto hangers she took down for that purpose, and everything else went into three additional hampers. They stood in a row against her wall, an accusing reminder that she hadn't even committed to this apartment enough to buy a dresser.

She rustled through one of the clean-clothes hampers and dug out a pair of nylon gym shorts, a sports bra, and a mesh running shirt. She had something social to do, for once.

Back at the office, Marcella had interrupted her perusal of the young men's phone records to invite her to Women's Fight Club.

"Fight Club?" Lei frowned as her friend, already changed out of her FBI outfit into athletic clothes, laced up her shoes. "What's that?"

Sophie Ang, hanging in the doorway, broke into a three-cornered grin. "Excellent idea, Marcella! We need some fresh meat down at the gym."

"Heard of mixed martial arts?" Marcella straightened up and picked up her gym bag. "It's kind of a hybrid of Muay Thai, Brazilian jujitsu, and boxing."

"I've heard of it, just not of chicks doing it," Lei said. "You're into this?"

"Hell yes," Marcella said. "It's awesome. Gets rid of work stress. Great workout, and it keeps your aggression-management skills up."

"I'm in." Lei suppressed a shiver of intimidation. She was smaller and leaner than either of the other women. One good punch would probably blow her away—but Tae Kwon Do and running kept her wiry and agile. She'd make them work for that punch.

"Good. Because there's a surprise for you there." Marcella's eyes sparkled with mischief.

"What kind of surprise?"

"Come, and you'll see." On that enigmatic note, her friend bounced out, Ang right behind her.

Ken waved Lei toward the door. "I'll close down here. Go. You need a workout."

Now, dressed for action, she looked in the fridge. Still nothing, dammit, and eating a burger on the way seemed like a good way to make herself sick. Food would have to wait.

It wasn't long before she was entering the huge aluminum warehouse that housed the gym. Large and dim, the interior was lit by skylights and spotlights on long cords dangling from a high ceiling. The air smelled slightly musky with a tang of something that started adrenaline humming through her veins. Two women sparring in the central ring caught her eye, but they weren't familiar.

A weight area dominated one wall, and the other was marked by square workout pads on the floor. Marcella and Ang, padded gloves on, were already warming up.

Lei understood the appreciation on the faces of those watching them. Marcella was magnificent, even in a pair of long, baggy nylon basketball shorts and a sports bra. Ang was the surprise. The tall computer tech was surprisingly muscled, golden-brown skin braised with kanji tattoos that encircled her upper arms and ran down the exterior of her sleek thighs. The pixie haircut that looked professional in the office enhanced an aura of streamlined power.

Lei moved in between a couple of other onlookers to watch.

The women circled each other, faces intent. Marcella opened with a couple of jabs, then a high kick, a move that had Ang grabbing her foot and flipping her on her back with a whoosh of lost breath. But it didn't end there. Ang followed up the advantage with a grappling hold, locked around Marcella's midsection like a python. Marcella thumped and heaved to no avail, eventually smacking the mat with her glove-protected hand, a signal the bout was over.

Ang let go and sprang back to her feet in a fluid motion. "I told you to knock off those high kicks unless you know I can't grab you," she chided.

Marcella hauled herself back up much less gracefully and spotted Lei. "Oh good. You made it. Let's take a break, show Lei the ropes, and you can finish kicking my ass in a minute."

"Sure. Glad you made it, Lei." Ang went to a nearby gym bag and brought back a pair of the split-fingered padded gloves the other women were wearing. "Let me introduce you to our coach and show you around."

"Sounds good."

"Oh, Lei—the coach is someone you know." Marcella grinned. "That's the surprise."

"Who is it?"

"I'm not saying. I don't want to spoil it. I'm going to do some cardio, warm up some more." Marcella headed over to a stationary bike.

Lei trailed Ang as she pointed her to the warm-up area, weight area, practice mats, and sparring ring. "Bathrooms and showers back here. We get three hours every other night for Women's Fight Club, when we get to use the practice area and ring exclusively. I think you'll like our coach—he's only part-time, but he's really helping the women's aspect of the sport get some good events and exposure."

Lei stood slightly behind her as she knocked on a door and pushed it inward. "Hey, Coach," Ang said.

A man turned around from a file cabinet to greet them. Tall and brown, with a shock of ruffled dark hair falling over his brow, dimples, and a white grin that faded at the sight of Lei, Alika Wolcott was the best of *hapa*, mixed Hawaiian and Caucasian heritage.

"Lei Texeira." He stuffed the file back in the drawer and slammed it hard. "This is a surprise."

"Hey, Alika," Lei said. He wasn't the only one surprised. She regrouped first, stepped forward to give him the awkward A-frame hug of people who've dated and ended badly. His hands barely brushed her shoulders before he pulled away.

"What're you doing here?"

"I'd ask you the same. Thought you were totally embedded in Kaua`i."

"You know each other." Ang glanced between them as she picked up on the vibe. "Well. Hey, that's great. Coach, Marcella invited her." Her delicate inference set the blame on Marcella as the culprit. "I'll leave you two to catch up. See you back on the practice pads, Lei." Lei hardly noticed her departure as she and Alika took each other's measure.

"Never thought I'd see you again."

"Kinda mutual there." Lei groped for something to say to the man she'd dated on Kaua`i before choosing Stevens in the end. "I went to the Academy, as you must have heard—and they posted me here. Small world."

"Yeah. Well, I—decided I needed to get off the rock, expand the business in a different direction."

"This sure is a different direction." Lei gestured to the vast barnlike space outside the office.

"Oh, no. Coaching is just my hobby. I own the gym building, though. Still doing real estate development, working with mostly apartment and office buildings now." He leaned on the desk, a pose that emphasized his chiseled shoulders and back. "When Marcella started coming here, I should have known you wouldn't be far behind."

"Well, they invited me. Thought I'd give it a try. I do Tae Kwon Do; that should help."

"Not necessarily." Alika's normal confidence reappeared as he pushed away from the desk, leading her back out into the main workout area and toward the practice pads. "A lot of MMA is groundwork. Got to be careful not to get into those high kicks. Your partner can take you down. Sophie is really good. You can learn a lot watching her."

They rejoined the group surrounding Marcella and Ang, who were back at it. Sure enough, Marcella tried another kick, and once again Ang caught her foot and upended her, following up with a grappling hold. Marcella yowled with frustration and took to whacking Ang about the head and shoulders, then burst out laughing.

"No." Alika looked down at them, hands on his hips. "Just no. No laughing in the gym."

This time Ang laughed, too. Lei withdrew to one of the stationary bikes against the wall, watching as the two women hopped up and began another round. This time Alika followed them, circling around, calling advice to Marcella, and finally she was able to win a round with formidable Sophie Ang.

A few minutes later, Ang trotted over to Lei. "Ready to go?"

"You know what? I don't think so." Lei wasn't in the habit of backing down from a challenge—but she didn't have the where-withal to get smacked down in front of Alika, who was still looking on, now coaching another pair of women. "Think I'll just do some cardio and call it good. This isn't my thing."

"Oh, c'mon. Lei." Marcella approached, mopping her flushed face with one of the thin gym towels. "Get out there with me. Or better yet, let Alika show you a few moves." She winked. "He might still be into you." Marcella had had front-row seats to their dating debacle on Kaua`i, something Lei still felt bad about. She wasn't ready to joke about any of it.

"Seriously?" Lei felt a flush of embarrassed anger burn her face. "Not funny." She got off the bike. "Thanks for the invite, Sophie."

"Lei—I'm sorry. I was just teasing." Marcella followed her as Lei strode toward the door.

"See you at work," Lei tossed over her shoulder. She beeped the truck open and hopped in, slamming the door.

The truck revved satisfyingly as she pulled out, but it wasn't until she was back on the highway that she felt the prickle of tears behind her eyes. She liked to think she wasn't usually so touchy, but the combination of Alika, their history, and the sheer physical beauty of Ang and Marcella had her on the proverbial ropes. She felt like a pale shadow of herself.

Lei missed Stevens and Keiki with a sudden stabbing pain, so acute she grasped the steering wheel, swallowing back a sob. Maybe it was just a stomachache and what she needed was food.

She pulled into the same Burger King drive-through and ordered a Whopper meal. What the hell—fat and carbs might settle her churning stomach. She chomped down the burger in a few bites, and it rested, an uneasy brick, in her belly.

Lei drove back toward her neighborhood, but the thought of the empty, depressing apartment was too much to bear. Passing her building, she kept driving, this time heading down into Wai-kiki. Her route took her past Kwon's apartment.

That crime could be her undoing—somehow she had to find out who'd shot him. Getting Kwon's shooter behind bars was the only way she'd be totally safe. But how could she investigate without stirring up Kamuela's interest? She rolled her windows down to take in the sight of tourists clogging Kalakaua Avenue as she munched the comforting greasy saltiness of fries.

Her cell rang and she checked it—Marcella. She let it go to voice mail. She wasn't ready to talk about anything yet, and she knew her friend would want to. One more person she'd failed—she wasn't much of a friend to Marcella, either.

She spotted a young man in a hoodie, attitude palpable as he shouldered his way purposefully through the wandering crowds. Something about him reminded her of the Smiley Bandit—youth, angst, and attitude now airborne. What was this unsub up to? Was he really some kind of modern-day flying Robin Hood? If so, she couldn't help liking him even more.

Her cell rang again—this time her father, Wayne Texeira, in California. They talked only every few weeks, so she put the Bluetooth resting in the brake well into her ear and answered it.

"Hey, Dad."

"Hey, Lei-girl. How's Honolulu treating you this week?"

"Okay." Lei thought of all she couldn't say to her ex-con father about her cases, her broken heart, her chickenshit moment at the gym—it would fill a book. "How's Aunty Rosario and the restaurant?"

"Same old, same old. We're planning a trip over, though, for Christmas."

"Sounds great!" It really did sound great—though she'd have to get some furniture for her apartment if they followed through and showed up in a couple of months. "Hey, Dad, it's a good thing you called. Remember the Charlie Kwon shooting?"

Her father was silent a moment, probably taken aback by the abrupt change of subject.

"'Course." His voice was clipped. He obviously still remembered her phone call to ask if he'd done it, too.

"Well, it's never been solved, and I'm starting to think I'd better work on it somehow. I visited him the day he was shot, you know, and I'm still worried it will come back on me."

"You told me then that you didn't do it. You have to let the facts be enough. Let sleeping dogs lie."

"I know, and you're right about that. But maybe there's some way I can point the investigation to the right answer or something—get some more insurance for myself. So I was wondering if you knew of anyone who might have been involved. Had motive, you know. Some of the Hilo people, maybe?" It was a long shot, but worth taking—and she'd never asked him since their abruptly ended conversation a year ago.

She waited the long moment he took to answer, driving through the stop-and-go traffic into the cool green of Kapiolani Park.

"Any number of people wanted Kwon dead," Wayne said. "But there's one I think you might want to get to know anyway. Your grandfather."

"What?" Lei pulled into the park's nearby lot. This surprise was going to take her full attention. She brought the truck up under a spreading monkeypod tree in the generous parking area. "You mean the Matsumotos?" Wayne and Rosario's parents were gone, so it had to be her Matsumoto grandfather. She hadn't seen them since she was a baby.

"Yes. Your grandfather Soga Matsumoto contacted me last year. He's been following your career from a distance and he lost track of you after you moved to Maui. He tracked me down, wanted your address, and said his wife died." Wayne sighed, a long, shuddering loss of breath. "I was pretty angry. They hadn't done anything to help you when your mom died and you almost went into foster care…I thought he didn't deserve that chance, and I told him off. I told him about Kwon, too, to make him feel bad."

"Wow." Lei felt the familiar tightness of anxiety and loss in her chest. Her family life had never been simple. She found her hand sliding into her pocket to retrieve the white-gold disc. She flipped it between her fingers. A ray of sunlight passed through the windshield, glancing off the embedded diamonds and casting sparkles onto the felted interior of the truck's roof.

"Yeah, I was angry. I wanted him to suffer, to feel bad for being such a bad grandfather. I have his address. I felt the Lord telling me my attitude was wrong later, so I called him back and apologized, but he wouldn't answer my call."

"And did you give him my address?"

"Yes. But I guess he never contacted you?"

"No. No, he didn't." And now her grandmother was dead and she'd never know her. Lei leaned her forehead against the steering wheel, closing her eyes. Somehow the unexplored possibility had been a little something she'd cherished.

"Well, maybe you could find him. If you felt like it." Wayne's voice had gone tentative. "I'm sorry, sweets. I should have contacted you when he got in touch with me, but I was worrying I'd mucked it up—and I've already mucked up so much in your life. I pray for you every day, you know."

"Thanks, Dad. It's okay. It wouldn't have made a difference, and I'm sure some rigid old Japanese man didn't have anything to do with Kwon's death. He'd never get his hands dirty like that."

"Your grandpa was a Korean War vet—decorated and everything. Maylene liked to talk about how hard he fought in the war, how he never accepted the military's bias against Nisei, Japanese. He's got a lot of the samurai in him." Wayne's voice was colored with respect. "I've always thought Yumi was the one behind them cutting us off. Maylene used to say she never did anything right for her mother and finally gave up trying."

"But it's a long stretch in any case."

"I agree. But you live in Honolulu now. He does, too, and he's a lonely old man. It's an opportunity; that's all I'm saying. That's what the Lord's put on my heart to tell you, anyway."

"You talk about God like he tells you what to do." Lei was never sure how to take her father's prison conversion—it seemed sincere because her aunt confirmed Wayne's involvement with his local church, his prayer habits and clean living.

"He does. It's a relationship, not a religion—for me."

"I do pray, but God doesn't answer." Lei closed her eyes, rubbed the disc.

"Maybe He answers, but you aren't listening. Scripture says it's simple: if you believe in your heart, and confess with your mouth that Jesus is Lord, you will be saved."

"Dad, I don't need saving." Lei pushed up off the steering wheel. "If God loves me, why am I so miserable? I gave up everything for this job, and I'm finding—it's not enough. I'm not even sure I want to stay with the FBI. Stevens got married while I was in the Academy. And he's got my dog."

"Oh, honey." Her father's voice sank. "I'm so sorry. I know you loved him. I thought you guys were together even after you left for the Academy."

"No. He told me he was tired of waiting because I wouldn't get married. So he married that Thai girl we rescued, of all people. And I liked her, too!" Lei felt her throat closing on the betrayal and coughed, clenching her fist around the disc until it dug painfully into her fingers. "I know it's not fair to feel this way—he never lied to me or led me on—but I guess I just didn't believe he'd find someone else. What we had was—special." Such an inadequate word to describe the passion, the camaraderie, the thousand shared moments that had healed her—and she'd thrown them away.

"God must have someone better for you."

"Not interested." She shook her head. "I need another man like a hole in the head. Give me my grandfather's phone number and address. I'll think about looking him up."

Wayne read it off to her, and she jotted it down in her spiral notebook. "You know, you could ask for Keiki back, Lei."

"Not a bad idea. Only, then I'd have to talk to him."

"For Keiki, you'd guts up and do it. That dog really *is* something special."

"I know. Thanks, Dad. And thanks for the prayers, too." She hung up. She'd never shared so much with him, and in spite of sticky moments in the conversation, she felt better.

Someone loved her. Three someones, if she counted her dad, her aunty, and if her grandfather really had been following her career at a distance, maybe he loved her a little bit. Enough to kill her molester? It was worth checking out, even if it was a long shot.

She was finally ready to go back to her claustrophobic apartment.

Chapter 10

"*H*ello?" Her grandfather's voice had a dry quality, like rubbing sticks together.

"Hello. Is this Soga Matsumoto?" Lei put police in her crisp tone as she sat on her couch, the white-gold disc on the coffee table in front of her.

"It is. What is this about?"

"This is Lei. Leilani Rosario Matsumoto Texeira. Your granddaughter." It felt important to say her full name, though her tongue tripped across its unfamiliarity.

"Lei." He seemed to be gathering his thoughts, adjusting. "I am happy to hear from you."

"Oh really?" She let the pause spin out, waiting to see what he would say next.

"Yes. You must have gotten my number from Wayne."

"I did. He says you live in Honolulu."

"Yes, out by Punchbowl." The extinct crater, site of the National Memorial Cemetery of the Pacific, was an easy, striking landmark in Honolulu. "I have a house. The same one your mother grew up in."

"Okay."

"I have been following your career. Congratulations on the FBI."

"Oh. Well. Thanks." Lei felt her throat close on all the questions—why hadn't they ever contacted her, found her when she was a child, when their daughter, Maylene, was descending into the darkness of her addiction? Why had they let her go to her aunt (though that had been the right place) without even a word or a card in all those years?

"I bet you wonder where we were all those years," he said, seemingly reading her mind.

"Kind of, yes."

"Your mother, Maylene, she was a great disappointment to us. To your grandmother Yumi, particularly. Yumi, she never did see eye to eye with Maylene, and she didn't want to seem like…" His voice trailed off.

"Like she approved of her choices."

"Right, as you say. And we lost track of Maylene after Wayne went to prison. I didn't even know what was happening until we had a call from the police department that she'd died, that you'd gone into foster care with your aunt. And Yumi, she said Maylene had made her choices."

Lei closed her eyes, reached forward to pick up the disc, rubbed it. She realized in that moment that at some point in the last few years, handling something when stressed had gone from a coping technique she needed to a habit. She set the disc down.

This conversation was way harder than she'd imagined. She wondered what the hell her father was thinking, bullying her into calling.

"But I never—I never agreed with it. I always wanted to find you." Soga's voice had a vibration in it—age or grief? It was hard to tell.

"Why didn't you?" Lei burst out, feeling the sting of tears at the back of her eyes, thinking of those early years with Rosario in California, a Hawaii girl getting used to a new school, teased for her unique, multiethnic looks. Even a birthday card, one of those sparkle-covered puppy ones, would have meant so much to her back then.

"Yumi, she had her ways." Suppressed emotion colored his formal tone with the richness of regret. "I should have contacted you anyway. I'm so glad you called, because I can say I'm sorry."

Lei imagined how hard it was for him to say those words. To a first-generation Japanese man of his age, such admissions were a sign of weakness—and proof she mattered to him.

"It's okay. It was what it was." A variation on the phrase her therapist Dr. Wilson had often used to help her accept the unacceptable.

"I imagine Wayne told you—your grandmother is gone now."

"Yes. And I'm sorry I never knew her." Lei cleared her throat around the tightness there. "Even if she never wanted to know me."

"It's not that." He sighed, a long, sad sound. "Yumi, she was proud."

"Well, I do have something to ask you. Something kind of hard." Lei straightened up a bit. Maybe he'd confide in her if she just came out with it, if she was vulnerable first. "Wayne told you I was abused by a man named Charlie Kwon?"

A swift intake of breath. Her grandfather hadn't expected that. "Yes."

"Well, you must also know his murder is unsolved. I have to tell you something." Lei steeled herself, picking up and squeezing the white-gold disc so tightly that the embedded diamonds dug into the pads of her fingers. "I visited him the day he died. To tell him off. Someone must have seen me—even though I was disguised—because they want to question a woman matching my description. I didn't do it, but if I'm questioned and my visit to him comes out, it will probably ruin my career."

A long silence ticked out between them. Lei realized she didn't know what he looked like. She tried to imagine a seamed, stern face that went with the voice, but nothing came into focus. She could hardly remember her mother's face either, and as always, she felt that mixture of sad and angry that thoughts of her mother brought back to her.

"I am sorry. I don't know what you think I could do about this," Soga said. The dry formality was back in his voice. "This situation is difficult for you, but I am sure you will be able to handle it. You've handled much worse."

"Yes, I have." She blew out a breath. "Yeah, I can handle it. Some crazy thing—I don't know—I wondered if you knew anything about his death."

"I knew that he died and that he deserved to die." There was steel in her grandfather's voice, and Lei remembered what her father had said: "There's a lot of the samurai in him."

"Okay. Forget I asked. I'm just stressed out. Maybe we can have lunch sometime."

"Yes. I have a favorite noodle house—I think you would like it." He gave an address, and she heard the relief at the change of subject. She gave a tentative time the next week, when she hoped the investigation would have simmered down to a manageable level, and said goodbye.

The jarring buzz of Lei's phone vibrating on the edge of the bathroom sink after her shower had her reaching for it even as she wrapped a towel around herself. "Hello?" She forgot to answer with her title, and winced.

"Lei." Marcella's voice breathed out a sigh of relief. "Thanks for picking up. Listen, I was an ass. Let me make it up to you."

"I don't think I'm up for going out tonight." Lei thought of the discos and neon-hip bars Marcella liked, how uncomfortable they made her feel. "How about you come over? I'll order some Chinese if you're hungry, and we'll have those Coronas we never got to."

"Good. Because I'm outside your door." Thumping penetrated as far as the bathroom. "Come on. Let me in."

Lei checked through the peephole before undoing all her security measures and letting Marcella in. Her friend looked freshly showered, cheeks flushed from the gym and long brown hair brushed back.

"Medicinal purposes." Marcella held up a bottle of white wine and a pint of Häagen-Dasz Vanilla Swiss Almond, Lei's favorite. "Anything else we eat is optional."

"Thanks." Lei took the items. "Now you get to see what a hole this place is. I was trying to put that off—like forever."

"It's not bad," Marcella said, looking around at the yard-sale futon and coffee table that were the extent of Lei's furnishings. "Needs a homey touch or two, that's all."

"C'mon. You saw my other place—the one that burned. I had a nice leather couch, paintings..." Lei's voice caught, and she turned away, tightening her towel. "There are some menus by the phone—why don't you call for Chinese? I don't need much. I had a burger after the gym."

Lei went into her bedroom and shut the door. She didn't want Marcella to see the bareness of her room. She dressed quickly, realizing as she did so that part of her reluctance to buy anything was that she'd never really mourned what she'd lost in the fire on Maui—all the furniture she and Stevens had purchased together, the king-sized bed she'd hauled to three islands, the paintings she'd chosen with such care.

It was time to get over all that, but this pathetic apartment just wasn't the place. She wanted her dog back, and to get Keiki, she needed to make some changes.

She came out, scrunching Curl Tamer into her damp, way-ward locks. Marcella sat in the corner of the couch. Two plas-tic glasses of wine waited on the coffee table. "Chinese is on the way. I haven't eaten since the gym, so there's going to be a lot."

"That's fine." Lei sat next to her friend, poked her in the biceps. "You could have warned me about Alika—it wasn't a fun surprise for either of us. I still feel bad for all that went down on Kaua`i with him."

"I realize that now—I was just thinking, Great, you need to get over Stevens, and here's a hot guy who was really into you and is still single…" Marcella took a sip of her wine. "I'm sorry. Like I said, I was an ass. I just don't do relationships well."

"Me neither, obviously. I haven't even had time to really let it sink in that Stevens is married. I mean, I'm just starting to realize all I threw away when I joined the Bureau. And for what? This?" Lei's gesture took in the bare walls, the cramped space.

"No. For this." Marcella leaned forward to tap the FBI shield Lei had taken off and set on the coffee table. "For great cases that take you all over, for a great team to solve them with, for all the resources the federal government can put behind you." She sat back and sipped her wine. "Local law enforcement is inherently limited, especially on Maui."

"Yeah, I know." Lei picked up her wine. "But I also hate all the bureaucracy, the structure in the Bureau. I mean, just yesterday, I had an idea, I followed up on it, and Ken got his panties all in a bunch over it." She described her drop by at the high school and the fact that Waxman was scrutinizing her.

Marcella snorted. "Waxman's been on my ass since he got here. You know what they call female agents? Split tails." She shook her head. "Rumor is, he's a misogynist. He second-guesses and double-checks everything I do, too. Sophie's the only female agent I've ever seen him praise, and she's so amazing, you'd have to be blind not to notice it. Seriously, we're just up against some garden-variety gender bias here."

The doorbell gave it's feeble, unfamiliar electronic buzz, and Lei got up, checking the peephole before opening the door enough for the delivery guy to hand the containers of food to Marcella over the security chain. That chore completed, they went back to the couch.

Lei scooped noodles up with a pair of chopsticks. "Guess I found a separate stomach with room for Chinese," she said. "I'm still just not sure if the Bureau is the right place for me long-term. But I have come to a few conclusions, and one of them is that I need a different place. I'm going to try to get Keiki back."

"Good for you," Marcella said. "I'll drink to that." They clinked glasses. "And if you aren't into Alika anymore, I'll tell Sophie to give him a workout. She's had her eye on him for a while." She wiggled her brows.

"Why don't you go out with him?"

"I'm actually sort of with someone. I'm not talking about it, waiting to see if I still like him in a few months before I say anything."

"Oh my God. Who is it?" Lei poked Marcella with her chopsticks. "You owe me a name."

"He's a detective with HPD. Seriously. I have such a bad track record, I keep waiting to lose interest, but I'm still having fun." Marcella grinned. "He knows what a girl wants. All I'm saying."

"Ha. Anyway, I'm surprised Alika hasn't been snapped up."

"Many have tried, or so I've heard." They gossiped about the various staff members at the Bureau; then Marcella asked, "So what's up with Ken? Is he single?"

"Seems to be." Lei buried her face in a white cardboard food container. "We don't discuss that kind of thing." She didn't like to miss a chance to dish to Marcella, but she was holding a secret for her partner—a big one. Partner secrets always came first, she'd learned in her years as a police officer.

"He's kind of—hard to pin down." Marcella rolled her shoulder. "Damn, this shoulder wound hurts. Did I ever show you my latest bullet scar? Remember the one that happened while you were in Quantico?"

"Oh, that's right! Show me!"

Marcella pulled her shirt aside so Lei could check out the dime-sized hole in her friend's shoulder, a divot of pinkish puckered skin.

"It's healed fine."

"Still aches, though. The bullet grazed the bone and hurt like a mother. So where are you on the case?" They reviewed everything they'd done on the case so far, including the fact that the unsub was now verifiably armed, and Marcella yawned. "I'd better get going. Are we good?"

"More than good." Lei hugged her friend. "Thanks for coming over."

The phone ringing dragged Lei up out of a restless sleep. She yanked it out of the charger.

"Special Agent Texeira."

"Lei, turn on your TV." Ken's voice was tense.

"I don't have a TV."

"Fuck all, really? Okay, you can catch this later. Apparently, the Bandit sent a tape to Wendy Watanabe, the reporter for KHIN-2 News."

"Whoa. What's the story?"

"Just get in here." He clicked off.

Chapter 11

*L*ei tossed off her blanket and dug herself out of the air mattress. She made good time to the Bureau office, noticing the brilliant sunrise breaking over Honolulu skies, an early breeze clattering the palm fronds, mynahs gossiping on the railings. It was only 6:37 a.m. when she slid into her chair at the conference table. Waxman had the retractable screen down and a shadowed figure, distinctly male, was talking through a voice distorter.

"It's not right for the one percent to live on our islands and give nothing back to the community. The Smiley Bandit is here to even the playing field, to give back a little something of what's been taken from our hardworking local people."

Wendy Watanabe appeared, a tidy blue suit emphasizing a petite figure, voice reporter-earnest as a background photo of the box on the steps of the Institute appeared.

"This was the recording that came into my e-mail inbox this morning from the burglar calling himself the Smiley Bandit, along with a link to this blog post. The burglary that occurred yesterday was the second in a series of bold break-ins, and the entire haul from that house was deposited on the steps of

Honolulu's biggest homeless shelter. Speculation is rife that the Smiley Bandit may be able to fly to the outer islands in the Hummel ultralight aircraft he stole from airline owner Max Smiley. Could this be a burglar with a heart? Police and FBI were not available for comment, but this reporter will be following the story exclusively."

Waxman snapped off the recording. "Full mobilization. I want every cop out there looking for any of our suspects, and let's reinterview anyone who might be able to give us a lead."

Just then the tricornered conference phone in the center of the table rang. Waxman hit Recieve. "Yes?"

"Call from Maui PD on the line, sir," NAT Greg said. Lei wondered how he always sounded so cheerful.

"Put it through," Waxman said.

"This is Captain Omura on Maui." Lei's former boss's voice was crisp. "We think we've spotted the aircraft you're looking for in Maui airspace."

"Thanks for calling. Please dispatch units to apprehend, and we'll send our agents ASAP," Waxman said.

"Already done. The aircraft was spotted flying very low over the north shore area. It could have landed anywhere, but we have several units out looking for it. Have your agents contact Lieutenant Stevens. He's heading up the team following this. Captain Omura out." Waxman looked up over his half-glasses at Lei. Even at six thirty in the morning, he was dapper, shaved, and pressed. "Texeira and Yamada, take the helicopter over there; liaise with the Maui people. Scott and Rogers will continue the investigation over here. We want an FBI presence at the bust, and take rifles and nonlethal ammo for the takedown. With all the media attention the Bandit's stirring up, we don't want any more negative press than we can help."

"Yes, sir," Lei answered, her stomach dropping at the thought of seeing Stevens again. Oh well. She'd just have to guts up and do it—and maybe she'd find a chance to ask about getting Keiki back

"Report in to me when you make contact with the Maui PD." Waxman retracted his overhead screen.

At their cubicle, Ken handed her a vest. "We know the kid's armed."

"I hate these things." Lei wriggled on the Kevlar and Velcroed herself in. "They give me claustrophobia." Her heart rate had already picked up dramatically with the news.

"So, go call your boyfriend." Ken packed his duffel with quick efficiency while Lei scrambled for her crime kit and anything else she could think to bring. "Hope you don't mind—Marcella told me the basics."

"He's not my boyfriend anymore."

"Your ex then. Get going—I'm getting the beanies, rifles, and the helicopter." Ken moved off quickly. Beanies—tiny, hard rubber pellets filling beanbags and packed into shotgun shells— were nonlethal but still packed a wallop when a suspect wasn't wearing body armor, and Lei fervently hoped there would be a bloodless takedown.

No time to overthink it. This phone call was going to be all business, Lei told herself. She walked to the employee lounge, shuffling through the contacts on her phone, her heart beating in slow, heavy thuds against the constricting vest. She poured some fresh coffee into a mug, chipped off some Coffee-mate with a spoon as the phone rang.

"Lieutenant Stevens."

"Congrats on the promotion." He'd been a sergeant when she left, and Lei was pleased at how steady her voice was.

"Lei. This must be your new number." His voice sounded rough. It was still so early; her mind flashed to him in bed, Anchara beside him, all golden skin and reams of black hair. She stirred the coffee with a loud clatter to drown out unhelpful imaginings.

"Bureau phone. I'm liaising with you about the plane-stealing unsub."

"You mean the Smiley Bandit? We're at the station watching Wendy Watanabe's latest installment. Apparently, she's in contact with the Bandit and he's promised her an exclusive when he's apprehended."

"My SAC, Waxman, is on that. My partner and I are getting our chopper in the air in a few minutes to come to Maui. What's the status of finding the aircraft?"

"Nothing yet." Stevens adjusted his tone to match her no-nonsense one. "We have five patrol units out combing the north shore and an island-wide high-priority BOLO out. Aircraft was spotted by a unit out by Haiku Station—it was heading north. The pilot might have tried to make it to Hana Airport, so we have a unit dispatched to watch there."

"It's an ultralight. All it needs to land is a hundred-foot strip of empty road or lawn. The Hummel has landed and taken off using a golf course, so don't limit the surveillance to just established airports—in fact I think the unsub will avoid those."

"Understood. Funny to hear you use Bureau jargon." Stevens's voice conveyed a degree of sarcasm. "Is it all you hoped for?"

"Is *she* all you hoped for?" Lei burst out, surprising herself as she felt rage blow a flush up her neck. "You don't have the right to ask me anything."

"Oh. So I guess you heard." He wasn't backing down either. "I told you how it was when you chose the job. I hope it keeps you warm at night."

"Fuck you, Stevens. I want my dog back."

"See you at the heliport. And keep it professional, Special Agent Texeira." His voice was icy, and he clicked off before she could say anything more.

Lei bit her lip hard on the expletives that bubbled up and tossed her mug of coffee into the sink with a wet crash. She restrained herself from throwing the phone after it.

"Everything okay here?" Of course Ken had to choose that moment to come in.

"Fine. Dropped my mug is all." Lei fished the mug and its broken handle out of the sink and tossed them in a nearby steel trash bin. "When's the chopper ready?"

"Ten minutes. What's the status over there?"

Lei told him as they headed out and got on the elevator for the rooftop helipad.

"Scott and Rogers are tracking Blackman today and interviewing Kinoshita. She was located at her mother's. They're following up with more HPD resources to try to track down Rezents and Matthews." The elevator opened, and Ken punched in the code that opened the steel exterior door to the roof. They stepped out into wide-open space.

Lei loved the rooftop, and for the dozenth time, wished she remembered to go up there more. She blew out a breath at the spectacular vista of downtown skyscrapers on one side, the unobstructed sea on the other. The sun was fully up, brazing the iconic view of Diamond Head with gold and twinkling diamonds off the windows. Fast-moving cumulus clouds added depth to the deep blue arc of sky. Feasting her eyes on the vista brought her heart rate back down, and she felt the flush of anger cool as the morning breeze caressed her skin.

The bold X of the helipad marked one side of the roof, a raised air-circulation shaft and an open shelter with welded aluminum seating marked the other. Lei and Ken had barely seated themselves when the thrum of the approaching helicopter, a black Bell JetRanger, brought them to their feet.

They trotted under the whirling blades and got in, Lei squeezing into the fold-down jump seat behind the pilot and Ken. She put on her helmet with its built-in comm unit and clipped into the chest harness as Ken stowed the black duffel bags of rifles and other supplies.

"Gonna be a bumpy ride," the pilot said as they lifted off. "Always a lot of wind on Maui, and it's up already."

Lei's stomach plummeted as the copter swung up and off the building, promptly dipping in a draft. She'd ridden in them many times since her first time with Alika Wolcott on Kaua'i, but the soaring, bumpy means of transport still thrilled and terrified. The chopper headed out for Maui, and Lei pressed her forehead against the curved glass window as they buzzed over the city, always the most vertiginous for her. Once over the ocean, the pilot picked a steady line at ten thousand feet and Lei turned her head to look out the triangle of window and scan the sea for whales.

The surface of the ocean was cobalt and foam-flecked, the wind fortunately behind them. Lei spotted the long gray outline of a humpback moving beneath them. She felt herself almost able to smile as a plume of vapor marked the huge creature's breath, and in a heartbeat more, they'd passed it by, the shadow of the helicopter racing along the water. The wonder of seeing the great cetaceans in the vastness of their ocean home always helped her put things in perspective. She shut her eyes, letting the roar of the rotors drown her apprehension about seeing Stevens..

Lei must have dozed off, because seconds later, it seemed, her stomach was swooping again as the ground accelerated toward them at an alarming rate. The copter wove in the wind and set-tled, one strut at a time. Kahului Heliport was a wide-open area next to the main airport, surrounded by acres of stored, parked rental cars, sugarcane fields dancing like hula skirts, and metal hangars.

Lei hopped out behind Ken, walking bent over beneath the still-whirling blades toward a couple of SUVs—one of them familiar. Stevens leaned on the hood of the brown unmarked

Bronco he'd driven during the time they lived together on Maui, and her heart seemed to stop beating at the sight of him. Gerry Bunuelos, one of the detectives from Kahului Station, stood by a black-and-white with a light rack on top.

Lei headed for Gerry first.

"Lei! Great to see you!" The wiry Filipino gave her the kind of shoulder-hug-backslap male friends exchanged.

"Likewise." Lei turned to her former fiancé. "Hey, Stevens. Don't think either of you have met my partner, Special Agent Ken Yamada."

The men shook hands, and that's when Lei let herself really look at Stevens—her eyes wandering up his rangy height. He'd put on more muscle—his long arms were thicker than she remembered. Laser-blue eyes looked at Yamada from a face whose rugged contours were more memorable than handsome as the wind ruffled his dark hair. Her heart was doing heavy thuds again.

She refocused on the issue at hand. "We need to let you guys know something important—wear Kevlar on this. The Bandit's armed."

"How'd that happen?" Bunuelos asked, as Stevens turned to her, his brows lowered.

"He took it out of the safe at the last hit. Walther PPK. According to the owner, no extra ammo was in the safe, but the gun was loaded with six rounds."

"That's a game changer," Stevens said. "Who else knows this?"

"We're keeping it under wraps as best we can. Don't want to create a situation," Ken said. "But you guys need to be apprised."

"I'll let the captain know, and we've got vests in the vehicles. So, Lei—we're taking you guys out to last-seen areas. Thought you could ride with me and Yamada with Bunuelos; we'll cover more ground split up."

"No," Lei said automatically.

Her partner narrowed his eyes at her. "Sounds like a plan. Give you two a chance to catch up."

Lei watched in helpless frustration as Ken walked away and got into the black-and-white with Gerry and they fired it up. Stevens opened the door of the SUV. "Well? Coming?"

"Shit," she muttered, and got into the passenger side. This couldn't go well.

Chapter 12

Lei slammed the door a little hard, and he slanted her a glance out of those blue, blue eyes.

"You know we have to talk."

"Where was the craft spotted?" Lei had chosen her tack—and it was to stick to business.

He turned the key and the Bronco roared into life. "North shore. We can head out toward Haiku. I know of some estates out there with lawns big enough to land on." He headed the Bronco toward broad two-lane Hana Highway, bordered by waving sugarcane. "So. You need to know something."

"I don't need to know anything. You don't owe me an explanation."

"I know I don't. I want to tell you anyway." His voice had gone as stubborn as hers. "Anchara was going to get deported. I couldn't let that happen, after all she'd done for the investigation, after all she'd gone through on that ship."

Lei turned halfway to look at his set jaw, mirrored sunglasses down and hiding his thoughts. "I'm sure it was a real hardship to rescue the beautiful sex slave."

"You know what? I'm sick of that shit, from you and everybody. Anchara doesn't deserve it, and you of all people know that!"

Lei did know that. Anchara Mookjai, twenty-four years old, formerly of Phuket, Thailand, had fled an abusive marriage to take a job on a cruise ship—only that wasn't what the contract had really involved. Smuggled on and off the ship in the ports of call, kept locked up on board, she'd found herself in any woman's nightmare—and had taken the chance for escape when it came. Her testimony had helped put away a whole layer of human traffickers working out of the cruise ships.

Not only that, but she'd proved herself to be a brave, resilient, and kind human being whom Lei liked more than she wanted to.

Lei turned and looked out the window. The view, of kiteboarders and surfers on the wind-whipped sea, green foothills robed in rippling grass, and the sweep of the twelve-thousand-foot Haleakala volcano, was familiar. She'd driven that route every day to work as a detective at the Haiku Police Station before she'd taken the opportunity to join the Bureau.

"I do know that. Anchara is…" Lei found her throat closing, and she swallowed hard. "She's a good person."

"Yes, she is. And she was getting deported, back to that abuser and the family who sold her to him. And you'd gone, with not so much as a wait-for-me commitment. In fact, you seemed eager to give my ring back and be done with me. Moving on to bigger and better things." He bit off the words as if they tasted bad.

"I had to do what I had to do." Lei set her own jaw. "But I never thought you'd do something crazy like get married! I mean—I know it wasn't fair, but I always planned to come back. For us to be together when I did."

"Same as before, right? Whatever suited you. No commitments. Well, I couldn't keep living like that. Anchara understands that."

"I can imagine." Lei let the bitterness into her voice. "And

I imagine she really shows how much she understands you. So you're not trying to tell me this is some sort of 'in name only' marriage, are you?"

"No. It's not. We're making a go of it." Stevens's mouth was tight, his hands white-knuckled.

Lei felt the last shred of hope bleed out of her—a balloon deflating, a weakening in the knees and guts, an utter draining of energy leaving nothing but a taste like ash in her mouth.

Stevens's hands clenched and unclenched on the steering wheel. "You know what? I dreaded this moment—but I feel better seeing you, knowing you haven't changed. Hope you're enjoying the Bureau and that it keeps you warm at night."

"You can bet I'm not enjoying it alone." The lie didn't sweeten the taste in her mouth, but the thought of Anchara in Stevens's arms, the way he obviously cared about her and defended her— she felt her chest constrict even further in the hot tightness of the Kevlar vest. Spots danced in the corners of her vision; darkness roared in around the edges. She pinched her leg as she heard his voice come from far away.

"I don't know why I tried to talk to you."

She leaned her forehead on the cool glass of the car window and concentrated on getting air into her lungs.

The radio crackled. "Come in, Mobile Unit Seventeen."

Stevens picked up the handset. "This is Seventeen. Over."

"This is Dispatch. We have a burglary in progress at 1879 Kai Huki Road in Haiku. Silver ultralight spotted in the area. Alarm company called it in."

"Roger that." Stevens hung up the handset. "Punch in the address on the GPS, will you?"

"On it." She leaned over to program in the GPS, using that moment of concentration to rein in her emotions. "It's only a few more miles up ahead. Turn right off of Hana Highway." She speed-dialed Ken's cell. "Did you get the call?"

"We're heading there, too." Ken's voice was tight with excitement. "Seems like we're closing in."

They roared down the two-lane road, lights flashing. Lei felt adrenaline replace the panic that had curtailed her breathing as Stevens cranked a right turn onto a long drive leading uphill and away from the ocean. Rolling pastureland dotted with light green palmate-leaved kukui trees opened up a vista on either side of them.

"Lots of open area to land," Lei said.

"Yeah." The radio crackled again, and Stevens picked up. "Mobile Seventeen here."

"This is Dispatch. We have two more units on the way."

"Roger that—anyone at the residence yet?"

"Negative, Seventeen."

Stevens glanced at Lei, eyes alight with the warrior gleam she knew and loved. "Looks like we'll be first on the scene."

Lei looked down, hiding the way that warrior light and the accompanying preraid adrenaline sent a pang straight to her libido by checking her weapon and badge as she scanned for the turnoff to the house. "Left here."

The Bronco's tires spat gravel as Stevens took the turn without braking, and they barreled down a narrow one-lane road lined with red ti plantings. Lei spotted a roof ahead, gleaming cobalt-blue tile. "There's the address."

They cranked into the driveway, roared forward—and came to a screeching halt at a huge iron scrollwork gate, shut across the driveway. A combination pad on a black metal plinth seemed to mock them.

"Dispatch, the gate is locked!" Stevens yelled into the handset. "Get us a code from the alarm company!"

"Roger that." Dispatch was dispassionate as always. Lei jumped out of her side of the vehicle.

"Gotta be a way over or through." She found a side gate disguised among the scrollwork, jiggled the handle as she looked up at the six-foot arrow-tipped black fence. Miraculously, the hidden handle opened.

"Stevens! This way!" He followed, both of them with weapons drawn, running toward a gracious-looking mansion built in descending levels down the grassy slope of a gigantic lawn. They were within a hundred yards of the house when Lei heard a sound like a sewing machine on steroids—a high-pitched bobbling whine.

"Son of a bitch!" she cried, as the Hummel appeared and bumped away from them, heading downhill on the lawn and picking up speed. It lifted into the air flawlessly, the sun gleaming mercury on its toylike, perfect airplane shape.

"Goddamn it!" Stevens shouted.

Stevens's cell phone rang. "That better be the goddamn code," he snarled. "Suspect took off right in front of us."

Lei didn't have the heart to follow him as he headed back down the pebbled driveway to open the gate and drive up to the house. She ripped open the Velcro and loosened the Kevlar, wishing she could take it off, but they still needed to check the house. Setting her hands on her hips, she watched the Hummel become a tiny silver speck and disappear over the treetops.

She trudged back toward the mansion as Stevens drove the Bronco up the driveway, closely followed by a blue-and-white MPD Crown Victoria and the black-and-white SUV driven by Bunuelos and Ken Yamada.

Stevens got out, still talking on his cell phone as he called in the BOLO for the Hummel and its general direction.

"Almost had him." Ken folded his arms and surveyed the acres of rolling lawn. "How many of these kinds of places are out here?"

"Too many," Bunuelos said.

"Well, let's get our kits and see what he left behind." Lei and Ken secured their crime kits and followed Stevens.

"If we'd had that gate code, we might have made it," Stevens said. "We could have used the Bronco to head him off."

"We'll get him next time," Lei said. It felt strange to be comforting him so close to their angry words, but familiar, too. She followed him as he opened one side of a magnificent fifteen-foot-high double door made of carved ebony inserts paneled in some exotic red hardwood. The hallway was polished cement, gleaming a dull metallic gray under their feet. They crossed scatter rugs of animal skin—giraffe, zebra, and before the massive fireplace of river stones set in cement, a snarling lion's head still attached to the whole hide.

"Very animal unfriendly. Hope the unsub found some good shit to take with him," Lei said. Animal abuse pissed her off almost as much as child abuse. She was respecting the Smiley Bandit more every day—his courage, resourcefulness, and choice of targets appealed to her, even as frustration dogged their pursuit.

"Let's check all the rooms. Spread out." Ken shot her a narrowed glance. Even in front of her old Maui compatriots, Ken was holding her to the high FBI standard that called for no unseemly joking or humor regarding the investigation. She tightened the Kevlar back down and followed him as he angled into a nearby hallway. Bunuelos and Stevens took the opposite wing.

It took a good half hour to search the sprawling mansion with its many subareas connected by cement-floored hallways and sets of stairs into each level. The combination of Balinese furnishings, African art and natural stone and wood superimposed on modern angles continued throughout the stunning design.

Lei and Ken found the heart of the house at last, a central and highly modern office. Stevens joined them at a cockpit of computers centered on a burled-wood desk.

"Homeowner says he had a safe in the desk," Ken said from his cell phone. Lei squatted down, opened a cabinet in the desk.

It contained a small safe, its door open, a loop of seed pearls hanging out.

"Looks like the Bandit figured this one out, too. What does the homeowner say about the combo?" Stevens asked.

"It's a cheap fire safe. This one looks tooled." Lei pointed to the scratch marks around the bent door.

"Homeowner Rick Rhodes confirms that." Ken turned off his phone. "They just kept five thousand dollars in there and some knickknacks for when they came on vacation."

Ken got an inventory list faxed and photographed as Lei got out the fingerprint powder. "Looks like he got away with a little more than five grand this time. Be interesting to see if he donates it."

"I want to see what food items he took." Lei walked back into the kitchen, a large bumped-out area off the great room, its towering ceilings pierced by skylights that let squares of sun onto the polished floor.

The familiar hook-mouthed smiley face grinned at her from the steel door of the refrigerator. Still gloved, she opened it. Stevens had followed her, and they both looked into the empty interior.

"Rhodes said it's not stocked," Stevens said.

"He'll be getting hungry then. Did they have anything in the pantry?"

"Some canned goods."

Folding louvered doors opened into a deep, shelf-lined room. A neat rack at the back held hanging cleaning tools. The shelves were stacked high with jars and cans of food, and Lei and Stevens moved in, scanning for anything apparently out of place.

"Dammit. This means he was able to stock up, though he couldn't carry much with him in the Hummel." Lei was painfully aware of Stevens's nearness in the narrow space, imagining she could feel heat off his body as he stood close. He's married and he loves her, she told herself firmly, but her knees were wobbly. Her heart pounded as she turned back toward him, a mere six inches separating them in the dim, spicy-smelling closet. "Nothing for us here."

Stevens's shadowed eyes lingered on her upturned mouth for a long moment. "I guess not." He spun and strode back out.

Lei followed, haunted by remembering the feel of their very first kiss—light as the brush of a moth—at a time when anything more would have scared her into running.

"Don't think this scene is going to tell us anything new," Ken said out in the great room. "What we need to do is keep the unsub running, keep the pressure on. Keep him from refueling, getting any food, and chase him into a corner." As Lei appeared, he gestured to his phone, held it up. Apparently, her boss was on speakerphone. "Agent Texeira and Lieutenant Stevens are present. MPD has been very helpful. We're getting on the road ASAP. The Hummel continued north, so it seems like he's headed into Hana. He didn't get much here."

They clustered around the phone, Bunuelos pacing a bit, Stevens with his brows pulled down, Ken with his samurai face intent.

"Get on the road, then. Push him off the end of the island. Out past Hana, there's nothing but the ocean," Waxman said.

"And the Big Island. If he makes if across the channel to Hawaii, he could keep us running for weeks," Ken said. "We'll do better keeping him contained on Maui if we can."

"Did he get any fuel at this hit?" Waxman asked.

Lei and Ken looked at each other. "Good question. We'll check the outbuildings and get back to you."

Lei took off out the front of the house at a jog. She couldn't wait to get away from Stevens and the overwhelming emotions he sparked—and she wished she didn't feel conflicted about catching the Bandit. She'd just have to work harder doing what needed to be done and hope it all sorted out in the end—but the questions nagged as much as the quest.

Chapter 13

*L*ei walked into the Kahului Station with its busy front desk and beehive of modular units. She paused on the way to the conference room to greet Abe Torufu. The Tongan giant hauled his bulk out of his chair to envelop her in a hug.

"Lei. So you decided to come down from the big leagues, show us some flash." He tapped the FBI badge clipped to her waist. Lei had never been so happy to see Bunuelos's partner—the big Tongan had always made her smile, and she badly needed both a hug and a smile.

"Good to be back." She shrugged out of the hot Kevlar at last. "Got an upstairs meeting, but I just wanted to stop in and say hi."

"You guys get the Bandit yet?"

"No, or he'd be following us in in cuffs," Bunuelos said, joining them. "Little bastard flew out just as Lei and Stevens pulled up to the gate."

"Well, check out the news." Torufu indicated a window streaming on his computer. Wendy Watanabe's sleek bob was doing a hula in an updraft of breeze with the control tower of Kahului Airport behind her.

"Shit, she's over here!" Lei exclaimed.

"Yeah. Not only that, but I guess the Bandit sent her video of his latest hit."

"We've got to talk to her. I better get to the conference room." Lei gave Torufu a wave and broke into a trot, not bothering with the elevator and hitting the stairs two at a time. Sure enough, the flatscreen in the conference room was tuned to the newscast, with Stevens, Omura, and Ken watching intently.

"This reporter has followed the Smiley Bandit to Maui, where he made a death-defying crossing from Oahu to Maui in a light aircraft not intended for this kind of distance. I received this recording in my e-mail." Watanabe's voice was rich with self-importance.

Lei watched a cockpit view as the tiny Hummel hit the turbulence that was such a part of life on the Valley Isle, bucking as the little craft bent in a northerly direction, following the curving line of bluffs that marked the edge of the island. Below the bouncing video, Lei could see the colorful arc of kiteboard sails. They watched as the little craft turned inland and headed for the cobalt-roofed mansion. It descended and made a perfect landing on the sloping sweep of lawn that skirted the house.

"We need that reporter!" Waxman's voice boomed, overloud, out of the triangular conference phone in the middle of the table. Captain Omura hit the volume button with a polished red nail. "KHIN-2 is refusing to muzzle Watanabe; I've been on the phone all afternoon. Find her in the field and get her working with us!"

"Yes, sir," Ken answered. Lei glanced around the table at the intent faces watching the camera view as the Bandit climbed jerkily out of the plane, set the Chihuahua on the ground, and followed as the little dog trotted toward the house. All they could see was a pair of Nike running shoes, the edge of denim jeans, and the sassy behind and curly tail of the tiny Chihuahua as it trotted toward the mansion.

"Max Smiley's going to burst a blood vessel when he sees his dog in this video," Lei commented. "Where's the kid getting intel on these houses? And which of our suspects has experience flying?" No one answered, but she felt better having voiced a few of the many questions.

The video cut to the office and the empty safe. Suddenly the same hooded, backlit figure appeared, the distorted voice speaking. It was clearly a switch to a totally different setting.

"The one percent makes another contribution. This time, five thousand dollars will be finding its way to dialysis patients at the Hana Medical Clinic."

Wendy Watanabe appeared again. "Until next time the Smiley Bandit, always one step ahead of the authorities, contacts me, I'll be reporting live from Maui. This is Wendy Watanabe saying aloha."

Captain Omura paused the feed. "Did your people have time to analyze that video?"

SAC Waxman answered from the conference call unit in the center of the table. "Our tech expert, Special Agent Ang, has been working on that. Agent Ang?"

Sophie's voice came through the conference phone clearly. "Yes, sir. It appears that the masked unsub making the recordings is the same one from earlier and in the same room. I'm checking the videos, and that's apparent. What this confirms is that we have two unsubs at work: one flying the plane and doing the robberies and one making the recordings. They must be in touch with each other."

"Any progress picking up the trail of any of our suspects on Oahu—Tom Blackman, Tyson Rezents, Lehua Kinoshita, and Kimo Matthews?" Lei listed the names for the benefit of the MPD staff.

"Scott and Rogers have been working with HPD and following up. So far, no leads." Waxman's voice was flat. "They found

Kinoshita and she alibied out. We need you to run that plane down. Did it refuel at that last stop?"

"Unfortunately, yes," Lei said. "I found a gardening shed that had been broken into, and the gas can for the mowers was empty."

"We circled all the way through Hana and came around the backside of the island," Stevens put in. "Nothing new."

"Well, track down that reporter. I'm working on a gag order from over here. Hopefully, I'll have it by the time you connect with her," Waxman said. "Thanks, Maui Police Department, for all your help."

"No problem," Omura said. "We have hundreds of eyes on the sky and possible landing areas. We'll get him."

The meeting broke up. Lei waved to Bunuelos and Torufu as she left the conference room, avoiding Stevens, who was studiously looking at a large island map pinned to one of the walls—she just didn't have the strength to speak to him. She'd been able to ride with Bunuelos all the way back around the island and hadn't had to spend any more time alone with him.

"Watanabe is holed up at the Maui Beach Hotel." Ken slipped his phone back into his belt holster. "That's handy, since that's where the Bureau put us up for the night."

"Good," Lei said. "Let's go get her." They climbed into a borrowed SUV and roared out of the busy station parking lot.

The Maui Beach Hotel, located in the middle of Kahului across from the mall, was a three-star establishment built in the 1980s whose main attraction was convenience. Lei and Ken checked into their rooms (double beds in lackluster pastel tropical print, rattan furniture) and reconvened at the bar, where the front desk clerk had directed them.

Wendy Watanabe perched on a bar stool in front of the mirrored bar, a five-foot powerhouse in a purple suit. Her cameraman had set his equipment on the floor near them, and both of them were blowing foam off pulled pints of beer. Lei settled herself on the stool beside Watanabe and flipped open her cred wallet for the reporter to see. Ken took the stool on the other side of the cameraman, a gangly young man sporting patchy whiskers.

Watanabe took a sip of her beer, expressionless. "Took you guys long enough to come talk to us."

"We've been busy chasing the kid. What do you call him? The Smiley Bandit," Lei said.

"He calls himself that." Watanabe took another sip, reached for a pretzel. "What can I do for you?"

"We'd like your cooperation in how you share info on this story," Ken said. "Barring that, we're working on a gag order."

"Gag order." Watanabe circled the rim of her stein with a finger, licked off the foam. "That's never gonna fly. And I'm simply reporting what the public wants to know—deserves to know. This is a great story, and the Bandit approached me with it."

"Sounds like you're a sympathizer." Lei realized she was hungry and barely stopped herself from reaching for the pretzels— but instinctively knew that eating in front of Watanabe would be a sign of weakness.

"Well, it's not like the kid's keeping the money. He's finding causes that deserve some attention and bringing that attention to them—even if they have to return his contributions. Did you know the homeless shelter brought in close to twenty-five thousand in donations in the days after the Bandit left that box on their steps?"

"Doesn't matter. The Bandit's a thief, and it's our job to catch him and lock him up." Lei felt defensiveness flare—a reaction to her own ambivalence. She hated shades of gray, and there were so many in this case.

"Hey, did it ever occur to you that this kid isn't hurting anyone? Taking a little loose change from the superwealthy, redistributing it to organizations that need it—how is that so wrong?" The cameraman, whose dangling plastic ID tag read CRAIG SALTZMAN, worked up some heat.

"That's for a court to decide," Lei said. "We can't have vigilantes and burglars trying to equalize society."

"Besides, there's the dog," Ken said. "It's almost like a hostage."

"You mean the little Chihuahua we saw in the video?" Watanabe asked. "That's what makes this kid a reprehensible criminal? There's been no hint of any threat against the dog."

"Wow, reprehensible is a big word." Lei gave back some attitude. "Trying to obfuscate the case with moral overtones doesn't change the fact that the unsub is breaking into houses and helping himself to whatever he can carry. We want access to all of your communication with the Smiley Bandit. You can spin this story any way you want when it's over and he's in custody."

A long pause while Watanabe and the pimply faced cameraman thought this over. "We'll keep airing whatever he sends us until we get that gag order," Watanabe said finally.

"There's another thing—the unsub is armed. He took a loaded gun from the safe of the Witherspoons' Kaneohe house. Just having that gun means he could use deadly force and changes the measures law enforcement will use to bring him in. So we need to take him peacefully, for his own safety." Lei wondered if she'd made the right choice telling the reporter even as the words left her mouth, especially as she felt Ken's sharp glance.

"Can I quote you on that?" Watanabe asked.

"No way. Probably shouldn't have told you. But we're worried someone's going to get hurt now—most likely, the Bandit." Lei realized as she said it how true it was, how much she really was worried the kid would get shot in the course of the chase—or, God forbid, create some sort of "suicide by cop" situation when capture was inevitable.

"All right, then." Watanabe drained the last of her beer and plunked it down. "I'll share what I have."

"Would you help us bring the kid in? Offer an interview or something?"

"You think I haven't already tried that?" The reporter snorted delicately. "Not that I planned to trap him—but I would have loved to interview him, backlit or something. But he flat-out refused. I'll forward the e-mails." She slid off the stool, bent over her shiny patent crocodile briefcase, and pulled out a laptop. "Give me an e-mail address to forward everything to."

"Why don't we do a clone of your hard drive?" Ken asked. "Then we can see what comes in as it comes in."

"No way. My computer's privileged."

Ken sighed as he told her the agency e-mail address, and Watanabe's fingers flew over the flat silvery keys.

"So he got my e-mail at the station, and he's been sending in the videos. There's been a little back-and-forth between us, but the IPs of each computer sending in the material are all over Honolulu—I already had our IT guy trying to trace them."

"Has he gone back to the same Internet café twice?" Lei asked.

"No. But there have to be two of them operating—the one flying the plane and the one making the videos—unless he's figured out how to have someone else just upload the videos for him after he sends them."

"An interesting conclusion." Lei was not about to add anything more than she already had to Watanabe's conjecture.

"So do you have a profile worked up on the Bandit?" Watanabe asked, slanting a look at Ken.

"This information flow is going to be one-way," Ken said. "Until we know we can trust you."

"I'm wondering what I'm getting out of all this." Watanabe wrinkled her pert little nose.

"I think you can be confident in having the exclusive inside track on the story." Ken glanced at Lei. "We have to check with our special agent in charge on Oahu, but it seems reasonable."

"Gee, thanks." Watanabe stood and tugged down her tiny purple jacket. "What a concession. So who are you looking at in terms of suspects?"

"You don't give up, do you?" Lei smiled. Persistence was a trait she'd always admired. "Why do you think the unsub chose you?"

"I cover a lot of youth events. I got my start reporting on high school football games and such. I think he must have become familiar with me that way. Perhaps I even interviewed him at one time."

Ken narrowed his eyes at Lei. "Get Ang on that," he said. Lei slid off her stool and walked out through the glass sliders overlooking the hotel's claim to fame, a wind-ruffled pool skirted in palm trees and cement. She speed-dialed the Honolulu lab.

"What's up?" Ang answered.

"Aren't you supposed to answer, 'Special Agent Sophie Ang'?" Lei said.

"Yeah. But I saw it was you. What do you need?"

"Can you pull up footage of Wendy Watanabe's youth reporting coverage on events? She thinks the kid might be someone she interviewed, or someone whose event she covered a few years ago before she switched to Features."

"Gotcha. I'll run a cross-reference with all employees of Paradise Air and their offspring."

"Great. That could help. Keep us posted." Lei punched off and went back into the bar. Watanabe and her cameraman were settling up the bill.

"Ms. Watanabe thought of something. A videotaped appeal to the kid to turn himself in. She says she won't need a gag order if we do that for her," Ken said.

"Whoa." Lei glanced at Watanabe. "What does Waxman think of that?"

"I've got a call in to him." Just then Ken's phone rang, and after a brief exchange, Ken hung up. "Okay, Waxman's all right with it. He wants you to do the recording."

"Oh shit, really? Me?"

"The new face of the FBI in Hawaii—young, female, and multicultural," Ken said. "Let's work out what you say."

Wendy Watanabe eyed Lei critically. "Got any makeup?"

Lei didn't dignify that with an answer as Ken pulled her aside. They jotted the main points Waxman had authorized her to cover and rejoined Watanabe and Staltzman, who were setting up a chair and portable light in one of the corners of the nearly deserted bar.

Lei sat in the chair and Watanabe sat in another one kitty-corner to her.

"I really have to touch you up." Watanabe reached over to button Lei's jacket. "Let's have your badge visible, too. If your boss wants you to be the "face of the FBI in Hawaii," we have to make you look good."

Lei's sweaty palms and racing heart weren't helping things any. She rubbed her hands on her pants, unclipped her badge from her belt and clipped it onto the slit of a breast pocket. "Okay. I guess."

Watanabe whipped out her makeup bag and touched up Lei's eyes with plum eye shadow, a flick of mascara, powder over nose and forehead, and finally, a raspberry lip stain. She sat back and admired her handiwork. "You should wear makeup more often."

Lei flipped open the powder compact and took in her changed appearance. She really did have big brown eyes and a nice mouth. Even her freckled olive skin looked better. She fluffed wind-frizzed curls. "Can you do anything about this, though?"

"Funny you should ask." Watanabe took another zippered

pouch out of her crocodile briefcase. "Shut your eyes." She spritzed Lei's curls with water and scrunched them with some sort of product.

Minutes later, Lei blinked into the mirror again. "Can I have you work me over every day?"

Watanabe smiled. "You learn a thing or two getting made over every day for work, but most of the time I'm in the field and have to do my own hair and makeup. So I've picked up a few things. You always have to put on a little more for the camera."

Saltzman had his camera on a tripod. He aimed at Lei and switched on the light. She was now looking into brightness, but she could see Watanabe beside her.

"Ready?" Watanabe asked, shuffling a couple of cards she'd been working on while Lei and Ken conferred.

"As I'll ever be." Lei straightened her jacket for the fourth time.

The little red light on the camera began blinking as Watanabe turned that high-wattage smile on. "Aloha from Maui. This is Wendy Watanabe reporting on the case everyone's talking about—the remarkable story of the Smiley Bandit. If you've missed it so far, the Bandit is a modern-day Robin Hood who began a burglary spree at the mansion of Max Smiley, owner of Paradise Airlines. Taking his moniker from Mr. Smiley, the Smiley Bandit stole an ultralight plane and has hit three houses, donating the proceeds to some worthy and relatively unknown charities." She turned that toothy smile on Lei. "With us today is Special Agent Lei Texeira. Agent Texeira, what can you tell us about the investigation so far?"

Already this wasn't what Lei was prepared for. Dammit, Watanabe was going to try and knock something loose on air. Lei licked her lips and tasted raspberry lipstick. "Well, we can't give out much information at this time. But we know that the unsub made it across the channel to Maui, and that's why we're here."

"And right away, the Bandit hit another house in Haiku." Watanabe shared the details of the burglary as Lei sweated under the light. She finally turned to Lei, extending the wand of her microphone like a scepter. "What is the FBI doing to apprehend the Smiley Bandit here on Maui?"

"As I said, it's an open investigation, so I can't comment much." Lei swallowed. "We have a high-alert Be on Lookout and a tip line established, so anyone spotting the aircraft, please call in. We are working closely with Maui Police Department personnel, and our first concern is safety for all concerned."

"What is the Bureau's position on the donations the Bandit has made?"

"The Bandit's gifts to charity are merely a gesture on his part, since the money and goods he's donated have been taken into evidence and are being returned to their rightful owners."

"That's not entirely accurate, Agent Texeira. Both Mr. Smiley and Dr. Witherspoon have chosen to let the donations stand, and it's likely today's donation to the Hana Dialysis Clinic will also be allowed."

"That's their right, of course." Lei narrowed her eyes at the smug reporter—more information Watanabe hadn't shared. She saw movement behind the camera—Ken working his phone, checking the facts. "Perhaps they weren't aware of these worthy organizations before." Lei straightened her jacket, looked straight into the camera, and tried to project warm and kind. "I'm here to ask the Smiley Bandit to come in peacefully. We are concerned for your safety."

"Safety, Agent Texeira? You've mentioned that twice now. What makes you concerned for the Bandit's safety?"

Watanabe was going to try to get her to admit the kid was armed.

"The ultralight is a very small craft, and accidents happen." A long pause as Watanabe continued to stare at her, the mike extended. Finally Lei said, "There are a lot of people involved in an investigation. We are relying heavily on Maui Police Department to help support us here on Maui."

"Yes. And we know there's a concern that sometimes police officers shoot first and ask questions later," Watanabe said triumphantly.

"I never said that! You're twisting my words. Smiley Bandit, if you can hear me, please turn yourself in!" Lei stood up. "This interview's over."

"Are you sure you don't have any further leads?" Wendy asked Lei's retreating back. "It seems KHIN-2 knows more than you do at this point."

"I have one further thing left to say." Lei whirled, put her hands on her hips, and raised her voice. "Gag order!"

"You heard it here first." Watanabe's voice carried across the bar after Lei as she stomped away. "The FBI plans to silence this reporter, and from then on all the public will know is what they decide."

Her voice continued, but Lei stopped hearing it as she stabbed the Up button repeatedly in the lobby.

"That went well." Ken spoke from beside her.

"Dammit, I lost my temper. Oh God. Waxman's going to have my head."

"At least you didn't give anything more away. And, hopefully, the gag order will come through before they run that story," Ken said. "We've got to get an early start tomorrow, and who knows what the unsub will get up to tonight."

"Ang's on the video thing." Lei stepped into the elevator. "She's cross-referencing any Paradise employees or their offspring in Watanabe's coverage."

Glum silence wrapped them as the elevator stopped at their hall, smelling of rug cleaner over cigarette smoke.

"See you in the morning." Ken slid his card into the door slot next to hers and stepped into his room. "I'll let you know what Waxman says tomorrow. No sense worrying about it tonight."

"Gee, thanks," Lei whispered as she entered her room.

She looked around—at least the room had a sliver of deck overlooking the pool, and she could see the twinkling lights of Kahului Harbor in the distance. Lei shrugged out of her light cotton jacket, hung it up on an empty plastic hanger, unbuckled her shoulder harness, and hung her weapon off the corner of the rattan headboard, unclipped her badge and set it beside the bulbous turquoise jar lamp beside the bed.

She felt a strange, nervy kind of exhaustion that reminded her she'd been through the adrenaline wringer more than once today. Smart thing would be to take a shower, order room service, watch some mind-numbing TV, and fall asleep.

Instead her mind turned toward Stevens. She imagined him watching the interview on TV, the way she'd been played. Raspberry-red lipstick was not enough to counteract how she'd been made to look a fool—and how she'd lost her temper. She mentally replayed her conversation with him in the Bronco, the tension—the pain of their meeting that had smothered her breathing.

God, it hurt that he was married. She wondered when it wouldn't anymore and couldn't imagine it.

In the bathroom, Lei stripped out of her dirty clothes and red-dirt-stained black athletic shoes. Water as hot as she could stand pummeled her tight neck and shoulders in the shower. She leaned her forehead against the cool tile and felt tears prickle her eyes. What a God-awful day.

She remembered her father's words: "If you believe in your heart and confess with your mouth that Jesus is Lord, you will be saved."

Maybe she did need a little saving after all, whatever that meant. Lei bent her head forward, warm water streaming over her head, down her face, washing away tears as they welled before she could feel them. Her lips moved even as she felt like a hypocrite: "God, help me. Please."

She scrubbed down briskly and turned off the water. There was nothing more to be done but go through whatever came next. What she really needed was a good night's sleep and to bring the Smiley Bandit in safely.

Somehow, some way, she felt a little better.

Lei blew on the surface of her hot coffee as she strode across the parking lot behind Ken to the borrowed SUV, on the way to their early-morning briefing at Kahului Station. She'd slept surprisingly well and felt rested and energetic. Her phone buzzed against her hip, and she slipped it out of her jacket pocket.

"Special Agent Texeira."

"Lei, it's Marcella. Listen, Ang came up with something. Both Rezents and Blackman were in high school sports—Rezents played soccer, and Blackman played football. Ang found video clips where they were each interviewed with a sound bite or two by Watanabe on KHIN-2."

Lei climbed into the SUV after Ken beeped it open and gestured to the phone, hitting speakerphone mode. "Sounds like a pretty strong connection. So maybe that's why Watanabe got chosen as the go-to reporter."

"Yeah. Not only that, but we have an early clip of Blackman doing a rant about the one percent. Ang ran voice recognition and it's a match to the guy in the videos, even with the distorter." Marcella sounded excited.

"Sweet," Lei said. "If Blackman's the one in the videos, he can't be flying the plane. That leaves the Bandit as Rezents or Matthews, or someone we haven't yet identified."

"Speaking of, we ran down Kimo Matthews. He's acting all surprised, like he doesn't know anything about anything. We haven't been able to get anything useful out of him."

"That's good, though. That leaves Rezents potentially flying the plane. We've narrowed the suspect pool at least. Do you think Blackman will follow him over to Maui?"

"Doubtful he'd come over to Maui given the BOLO at the airports on all those names."

"We're headed over to Kahului Station. Can you send a link to Ang's work on the voice recognition? We'll share it with the MPD team," Ken interjected.

"You got it. Waxman is sending us over today to help you guys," Marcella said. "Matthews has lawyered up, so we're keeping him in custody but need to take a break on the interviews. Waxman said he'd take over on that."

"Did Waxman get the gag order for Watanabe and the TV coverage?" Lei asked, trying not to sound anxious.

"He's trying, but the judge has also had an appeal submitted by KHIN. So he hasn't signed it yet. Why?"

"Because I mistakenly filmed an appeal with Watanabe for the kid to come in. It turned out to be a setup. The Bureau, and me in particular, look like idiots."

"Shit," Marcella said. "Oh, Lei, I'm sorry." Silence filled the SUV; then Ken turned the key and the vehicle roared into life.

"Call us when you get here." Lei punched off.

Maui's version of early-morning commute traffic was in full swing. They entered the flow of pickups, sedans with surf racks, and pineapple trucks to drive the short distance to the police station.

"I bet that bitch runs my interview on the morning news," Lei said glumly. Ken gave a terse nod.

Chapter 14

*A*rriving in the conference room for the joint briefing, Lei was dismayed to see a large flatscreen mounted on a wheeled cart filled with her own image. In the newscast, she sat in the rattan chair, her tilted brown eyes magnified by unfamiliar plum eye shadow and the raspberry lipstick that had been pretty in person rendered garish in the portable spotlight. That light seemed to highlight every wrinkle in her jacket and springing curl. Watanabe looked polished and collected in contrast.

They'd reached the point in the interview where Lei stood, told the kid to turn himself in, and then spun and stomped away with a pause to yell "Gag order!"

Lei's cheeks and neck burned with the blush that had been the bane of her existence for many years. She yanked out a molded plastic chair and sat, unfortunately next to Michael Stevens, who turned to her.

"Reporter's got game," he said.

"Yeah. And I don't," Lei said, watching herself walk away onscreen, looking temperamental as she jabbed the elevator button repeatedly while Watanabe's voice-over droned a repeat of the case. The hairs on her arms stood up in response to Stevens' nearness.

Captain Omura, her sleek bobbed hair and brass gleaming, turned the TV off with a click of the remote. "Good morning, Agents Texeira and Yamada. Hope you slept well after that fun interview."

"Not really." Lei looked around the table at the variety of expressions. "I never should have fallen for that. Hopefully, we'll get the gag order today. We do have some news, though."

Ken held up his smartphone. "Can I e-mail you some links? Our tech department found some important information."

"Of course."

Ken forwarded to the links from Ang to Omura, who hit the projector button and rolled down a screen behind her head. A screen shot of the voice recognition software came up, with matching points highlighted. "Agent Ang says these matching points identify the video messenger part of the Smiley Bandit as Tom Blackman, within a seventy-five-percent certainty."

"So who's flying the plane?" Omura asked, pouring herself a cup of coffee from a white plastic carafe and pushing it toward Ken and Lei.

Lei picked it up, poured some into a Styrofoam cup. She never used to be this addicted to coffee. "That's the million-dollar question, isn't it? We think there's a good chance it's Tyson Rezents because Ang also found video where both Blackman and Rezents, as high-school athletes, were interviewed by Watanabe. So that's a connection, and they both worked at Paradise Air and are young and angry. We think it's a strong assumption."

"Something you missed," Stevens said. Lei could feel his presence beside her, raising the hairs on her arms with his nearness. "Watanabe called some child advocates and told them the kid is armed and we are preparing to use deadly force against him, and they've been calling our station. If it's Rezents, that could be a problem since he's still a minor. Blackman is at least over twenty-one."

"Yes." Omura punched a few buttons on her computer, and a series of messages from advocacy groups scrolled up the screen. "These are from Twitter and e-mail. The *Maui News* has already called wanting comment on our plans to take down the Bandit, how we're going to avoid using deadly force. The kid's got his own fan page on Facebook, for godsake. He's being touted as some kind of modern-day Robin Hood."

Lei felt the ambivalence she'd been struggling with all along rise up. Did she really want to capture this brave boy, flying a tiny plane across the ocean to steal from the rich and give to the poor? Good thing her job was clear—catch a lawbreaker. How and why were for a court to decide, she told herself firmly.

"We've got to remember something the general public has forgotten. Even a twelve-year-old with a loaded gun is somebody who knows the difference between right and wrong. If he's a threat to me or other people who should go home at the end of the day, he needs to be stopped. That's the mentality we have to have. I'm not going to try and reason with a bullet." Stevens's jaw was set, blue eyes intense under those dark brows.

"That's certainly true," Ken agreed. "But given the PR nightmare and publicity of this chase, my SAC is calling for beanies and SWAT for the final takedown. We're all to carry rubber ammo just in case."

"The Robin Hood thing isn't helping us. I'm sure that's exactly the image he intended when he began feeding information to Watanabe." Lei held the disc under the table, where Stevens couldn't see it. "Of all the mistakes I made, leaking the gun thing to Watanabe is the most damaging. I expect to face disciplinary action when I get back to Oahu."

"Let's move forward with what we have to do today." Ken's averted, stony face confirmed that he'd already heard from Waxman to that effect. "Two more agents, Scott and Rogers, are on their way over, and we are all to switch to rubber ammo. Capture is the goal."

"Good. I'm glad to have something to say to the press and those child advocates," Omura said.

Just then, the triangular phone in the center of the table rang. A tinny voice came through when Omura punched the Receive button. "Captain, this is Dispatch. The aircraft has been spotted in West Maui, near Kaanapali."

"Any other details?" Omura asked.

"No, ma'am. It was flying over Lahaina, headed for Kaanapali. That's all we have at this time."

"Send all available units to try to apprehend. Beanies only," Omura said, as Ken and Lei stood along with Bunuelos and Stevens. "Get on the road, everyone."

"Ken, let me drive. I lived here, you know," Lei said as they trotted through the station behind Bunuelos and Stevens, with a stop to pick up department-issued rifles and boxes of beanies. He nodded, tossing her the keys as she speed-dialed Ang.

"Agent Ang, do you have any idea how he's choosing his targets?" Lei asked as they reached the SUV and she beeped open the vehicle, getting behind the wheel, Ken climbing in the passenger side.

"I've been working on that," Ang replied. Lei put her phone into the cupholder and set it on speakerphone. "I've got a couple theories based on the houses the unsub has hit."

"Good, because he's headed toward Kaanapali, and there are a lot of rich houses out there."

"Okay, I'll get right on it and try to send you some likely addresses."

"Thanks." Lei pulled the vehicle out behind Stevens's Bronco.

Cop lights on, weaving through town—it brought back memories, some of the happiest times of her life in hindsight. She wondered where Keiki was and missed her dog with an ache that felt physical.

They were on the Pali in no time, roaring along a two-lane highway around swooping cliffs above the ocean on the way to Lahaina. Wide-open vistas of cobalt sea marked by the lavender smudges of Lanai and Kahoolawe Islands and punctuations of whale spume might have distracted her on another day—but she was too busy focusing on driving at well above the speed limit on a road famous for accidents. Ken spent the drive on the phone with Waxman, bringing him up-to-date.

By one in the afternoon, Lei was hot, bothered, and hungry from fruitless searching when they rendezvoused with Stevens and Bunuelos at a little Mexican place in a strip mall outside of Kaanapali, still unable to locate the Hummel.

Lei tossed her Kevlar vest into the SUV as they went into the cantina. "Supposed to keep that on," Ken said.

"I can't handle how hot it is. The Bandit is not going to come in here for a burrito," Lei snapped. Inside the dim and slightly cooler interior decorated with dusty piñatas and embroidered tablecloths under glass, Stevens and Bunuelos were already perusing laminated menus.

"We're waiting on a list of possible targets from our tech agent, Agent Ang." Ken sat down in the booth across from the detectives, Lei beside him.

"Okay," Stevens said. "As you know, even with a full BOLO out and all our patrol cars on alert, no one's spotted the Hummel since it made an initial pass in this direction. Must have landed already."

"Probably ripping off a mansion as we speak," Lei said. "Not that I can blame the kid."

"You sound like you want him to get away," Stevens said as he looked at her. "Kid's a thief, plain and simple."

She hid behind her menu, wincing at hearing her own words come back to bite. "Nothing's ever plain and simple. I can't help liking this kid. He's brave, he's following his convictions. I'll do my job, but I don't have to like it. What's good here? We should eat fast and get back on the road."

"The enchiladas are good," Bunuelos volunteered.

They ordered, and Lei sucked down half her glass of iced tea, wishing it were a Corona and wondering what was in store for her when she got back to Oahu and met with Waxman. Some sort of write-up was likely the least of it.

Lei and Ken's phones toned at the same time, and they looked at them to see the list from Ang, along with a brief message: "The unsub appears to be looking for wealthy off-islanders with a history of bringing in nonlocal help and no record of contribution to the community."

Those were the kind of people Lei and so many locals resented. Lei's fish tacos and the rest of the orders appeared at that moment, and they dug in quickly as Ken forwarded the list to the two detectives' phones.

"It'll go faster if we split up and hit these addresses," Ken said. "I think we should keep the interagency partnership thing going, so Bunuelos, you're with me. That'll help me navigate a little better."

Lei sneaked a look at Stevens's face, dark lashes down over his eyes as he focused on his plate. "Stevens, I'll drive since I left my vest in the SUV we're using."

"Thought you were supposed to keep it on," he said without looking at her. "Still taking risks, I see. Thought FBI procedures were stricter."

"I'm her mentor, and I'm trying." Ken grinned, a glimpse of humor. "But as you know, the girl doesn't like protocol."

"That hasn't changed, then."

"Hey," Lei protested. "I made it through the Academy. I made it through probation. Remains to be seen if I'll make it through this case, though."

They wrapped up the meal and divided the list of addresses. Lei felt Stevens's eyes on her back as she practically ran to the SUV and hopped into the driver's seat.

He got into Ken's side. "Put your vest on."

"Shut up. You're not my mother." She felt childish for rising to the bait even as she complied, tugging the confining Kevlar down and Velcroing it into place. He was already programming the nearest address into the GPS.

They got on the road with just the lights on and in no time were pulling up to a lovely wrought-iron gate decorated with carved metal birds-of-paradise. Lei rolled down the window and pressed the button on a speaker next to the keypad. "This is the FBI. Open up your gate, please."

Excited squawks from the speaker, denials of a problem, but Stevens and Lei insisted on checking the grounds. Eventually, the artistic gate swung inward to admit them to a gracious estate, plantings lining a curving driveway that ended at a house doing a good imitation of a Japanese temple.

Lei suppressed her annoyance as they tramped around the estate, escorted by a caretaker, verifying that there was no evidence the Bandit had landed anywhere on the grounds. Looking out at the stunning view of Molokai and Lanai, separated by ten miles of open, sparkling ocean, she could feel a tiny bit of the anger at the world the kid lived in—a world light-years away from this one.

Lei wondered if she'd ever have had the courage to do something about that anger, like this kid was doing. At the same time, she knew that, in her way, she was trying to make the world a better place—even if it meant bringing the Bandit down.

They got back into the SUV. Lei loosened the vest again, glanced over at Stevens. "Where next?"

"We have two more addresses to check." Stevens punched the next one in. "So. You said you wanted Keiki back."

"Yes. I do."

"Turn left in six hundred feet," the GPS intoned.

"Want to see her? We can swing by the house on the way back to the station tonight."

Lei's hands went sweaty on the wheel as she tried to concentrate on the road. "'Course I want to see Keiki. But I don't want to see your wife." She tried not to choke on the last two words.

"She's not there."

"What do you mean?"

"She's visiting a friend."

"What?" Bumps on the median had her swerving back into the proper lane. She glanced over at him and noticed what she'd ignored so far—dark shadows under his eyes that just made them bluer, beard stubble, tufts of misdirected hair from his habit of running his hands through it when stressed.

"Yeah." He stared out the windshield. "We're working some things out. I don't want to talk about it."

"No way. You have to tell me what's going on." Black spots swirled around the edges of Lei's vision, telescoping it down—a return of PTSD symptoms she hadn't had in months.

"Turn right in three hundred feet," the GPS intoned. Lei yanked the wheel over and pulled up under a kukui nut tree on the side of the road. She tore off her seat belt, smothering in the tight, hot Kevlar vest. She wrestled out of the vest, gasping for air as she got it off her head. The black spots of incipient oxygen deprivation receded and tunnel vision opened up as she tried not to let herself hyperventilate.

"Still having panic attacks, I see." Stevens's voice was carefully neutral as Lei did her relaxation breathing: *In through the nose, out through the mouth. In through the nose, out through the mouth.* She put her head as far forward as she could, given the steering wheel.

"Obviously. They were better though, until today." She felt her heart rate coming down and turned to him. "What's going on with you two?"

"You're the last person I should be talking to."

"I'm the first person, since you never should have married her." A desire to hurt him like he'd hurt her made the next question burst out. "Did you hit her or something?"

"No. God no. I can't believe that's where your mind goes." He picked up the department-issued Remington 870 twelve-gauge, cracked open the loader, and checked that the beanie cartridges, marked hot pink, were loaded. Ratcheted the gun with a sound that instinctively raised her heart rate again. "She's upset since I've been in touch with you."

"What do you mean? It's the case. It's all business. It's obvious you wouldn't have anything to do with me if you could help it." She tried not to sound bitter and was pretty sure she'd failed as he narrowed those blue eyes at her.

"Apparently I 'haven't been myself' since we've been on this case. She said she needs some space to think about things and wants me to do the same."

He wasn't himself. He still felt something for her. Lei wanted to think on what this meant but her cell toned, and she grabbed it out of the cupholder. "Agent Texeira here."

"Lei, it's Ken. We aren't finding anything so far."

"We aren't either." She started the vehicle and hit her Bluetooth, pulling them back onto the narrow side road. "We've only been to one of the addresses, though. This is kinda inefficient."

"I know, but at least Ang was able to find enough commonalities to give us something to check. Let me know when you're done with your list."

"Of course." She clicked off as the GPS gave the next direction and glanced at Stevens. He had the second shotgun open on his knees and was ramming the hot-pink beanbag shells into the chamber.

"So what're you going to do?"

"Nothing."

"What do you mean? You should go after her."

"She said she needs space to think. I'm giving it to her."

"That's womanspeak for, "I want you to prove you love me and come after me.""

"I don't know about that." He shut the loader with a click and laid the gun on the backseat with the other one. "She's from Thailand. Maybe it means something different there."

"It doesn't. Even if she gets mad when you go after her, she's doing this to test you. See where your loyalties lie. And damn if I can believe I'm giving you marriage advice." Lei shook her head as she pulled into another gracious driveway bisected by a grand-looking metal gate. "Do whatever; it's nothing to me." She tried to say it like she meant it as they rolled down the drive, eager to change the topic. "Didn't know there were so many of these fancy gates over here. Metalworkers must be doing okay in this economy."

It would always be part of Lei's experience to identify with the workers who built the houses and kept up the estates more than those who occupied them. She'd had to work too hard just to drive a decent car to ever forget the divide between the wealthy and working class in Hawaii, a state run on a service economy.

They went through the admissions and explanation process three more times before they'd run out of the list, and after checking with Ken, decided to head back toward Kahului in the cooling light of evening—the Bandit must have gone to ground, because even with the island-wide BOLO, no one had spotted the ultralight again.

"So do you still want to see Keiki?" Stevens asked, as they

came around the last of the curves of the Pali toward Kahului, the main town spread out through the waist of the figure-eight shape of the island.

"Of course. And I want her back. I'm serious about that." She angled a glance back at him. "I'm not liking my shitty little apartment on Oahu. If you'll bring Keiki over, I'll get a proper place."

"Seems like both of us wanted some things that didn't work out," Stevens said. A world of regret colored that understatement, and Lei kept her eyes on the road, trying not to show her inner turmoil, as he pointed out a few turns.

He and Anchara had a nice, newer ranch-style home in the development of Wailuku Heights. Lei wound through a neighborhood complete with kids on bikes, speed bumps, and white picket fences, a sight that made her gut tighten with a conflict of longing and claustrophobia.

Keiki barked a familiar Intruder Alert as Lei pulled the unfamiliar SUV into Stevens's poured-concrete driveway decorated with urns of potted palms. She was relieved it didn't look anything like the little old plantation cottage she'd shared with him in the past—but the air of domesticity filled her mind with imagined scenes she could do without.

Lei opened the car door, and Keiki spotted her. Instantly, the big dog's menacing tone changed to happy cries as she leaped up, paws on the fence, hind end waggling frantically. Lei felt love surge up in her, total and unreserved, as she ran to the five-foot picket fence and took Keiki's big square head in her hands, gazing into the dog's intelligent brown eyes.

"I'm sorry I left you, baby."

"Nice to see you show some feelings." Stevens' voice was tight as he opened the gate for her, and Lei hurried in and went down on her haunches, hugging Keiki around the sturdy neck as the big dog sat, swiping Lei with her tongue. Keiki flopped in total submission, and Lei rubbed her belly. She traced the old track of a bullet that had gone into the glossy shoulder and left an ugly hairless exit scar on the dog's side.

Stevens reappeared with a couple of Coronas.

"We still have to drop by the station so I can pick up my car. You look like you could use a beer."

"A beer is great, thanks. Is Anchara still gone?"

"Yes. I'd invite you in, but…"

"I don't want to come in," Lei said quickly.

"Right," Stevens said. They drank, wordless.

Lei folded her legs to sit in the neatly trimmed grass, Keiki's head pillowed on her thigh as she looked around at the immaculate slice of suburbia, feeling like an invader, as if her presence polluted the dream of this middle-class paradise. The dog's eyes closed in ecstasy as Lei played with her silky ears. "You haven't said you'd bring Keiki over to me on Oahu."

"I love her, too," he said. "But seeing you together, I can't keep her. Let me know when you have a proper place, and I'll bring her over."

"Thank you," Lei said, gazing into his eyes for a long moment. They'd gone gray with shadows. "We'd better get on the road."

Stevens said nothing as Lei bade the dog goodbye, nothing as they drove back to the Kahului Station, and nothing as she let him out at his vehicle but "See you tomorrow."

No, there was nothing to say. But that night, in her lumpy Maui Beach Hotel bed, she fell easily asleep for the first time in months.

She was getting Keiki back. It was something.

Lei woke abruptly, sitting up, her heart thundering, covers tangled around her perspiring waist—a terrible severing from a nightmare that was born in memory.

Kwon on his knees before her, her hands, covered by yellow

rubber cleaning gloves, holding her Glock, wobbling and weaving as she took aim. In the dream, she'd pulled the trigger—and he'd flown backward, brains splattering the wall behind him in a Rorschach pattern of revenge that couldn't be undone.

Thank God she hadn't pulled the trigger that day, a day so emotionally loaded she still remembered the sight of the gun trembling, Kwon on his knees before her, his eyes shut tight as he waited for her to end his sorry life.

That position of power hadn't done a thing to bring back her childhood innocence. She hoped the clothes she'd worn for that confrontation, a platinum-blond wig and hot-pink jean jacket, were still where she'd hidden them in case she ever needed to produce them to clear her name. She wished she could find out who'd done it—only she didn't have a single lead or any time to pursue the case. And then there was Detective Kamuela, questing about for answers.

A run was in order. It was only five thirty, and she needed to sweat off the nightmare. She pulled on her running clothes and slipped out of the hotel, her feet picking up a familiar rhythm on the sidewalk through town. She turned toward the towering mass that was Haleakala, just beginning to be gilded by early-morning sunshine on the eastern side, a vast purple dormant volcano looming over the city nestled in the curve of Kahului Harbor.

The road, an artery through town, curved past a wetland bird sanctuary, and there was little traffic in the pearl-gray dawn. Towering, graceful cumulous clouds reflected in the still waters of the marsh. Hawaiian stilts with their long red legs picked their way across the flats, bodies still but for their darting heads searching for prey. Reeds stood still as rapiers planted in the mud bottom, and a scent of brackish algae wafted over Lei as she jogged beside a chain-link fence separating the town from the reserve.

At the corner of Dairy Road and Hana Highway, a big intersection with multiple lanes, Lei leaned over and stretched, stood, and when the light changed, she hurried across the intersection toward the familiar edifice of Marco's Restaurant. The black-and-white-themed Italian restaurant was bordered by a parking lot and red-flowered hibiscus hedge, and as she jogged across the lot she spotted Stevens's Bronco with the surf racks.

He was having breakfast at Marco's, something they'd often done before work when she was with MPD. Maybe she could get a coffee with him. Her heart went into overdrive, and it had nothing to do with running.

Just when she thought she'd accepted the situation, she realized she never had. Never would.

Lei's feet seemed to turn by their own volition to the glass door of the restaurant, and she pushed the handle and went in, stopping at the hostess station and rack of bakery goods, scanning the black-and-white booths.

That's when she spotted them.

Chapter 15

From her spot in the doorway, their booth was straight ahead against the far wall of windows. Stevens and Anchara were deep in conversation, their eyes on each other, each of their profiles as clear to Lei as if stamped on a coin that would stay in her memory forever: Stevens's high forehead, rugged jaw, and intense blue eyes on his wife, his hand holding hers on the tabletop, saying something as he leaned toward her. Anchara sat straight as a ballet dancer across from him. Her tawny skin, large dark eyes, and full lips were a sweet contrast to the fall of long black hair rippling over her shoulders.

She was as beautiful as ever. Maybe more so.

Lei felt that sensation she'd had before, an actual stab of pain to her chest that left her breathless. *Apparently a broken heart feels like a heart attack.* The thought rose from her mind, feeling alien and disembodied, hovering over her head, a stray conversation balloon, even as she turned and stumbled back out through the door, terrified they'd see her.

Lei got on the road again, hardly noticing where she was going, her eyes dry and unblinking. Somehow she ended up back at the

Maui Beach Hotel, autopilot a homing device as she showered and dressed.

The feeling in her chest returned now and then as she got ready for the day, a sliver of ice inserting itself into her breathing—but for the first time in her life, she didn't try to avoid or suppress the pain, and she was even aware of that.

She had a broken heart, and she'd earned it. She deserved it. She just needed to endure it until it got better and get to work anyway.

Dr. Wilson would be proud of her. Not that that changed a damn thing or made any of it hurt any less. Still, she was glad, fiercely glad, that she hadn't once thought of cutting herself over this.

Lei's phone rang. She picked up to Ken's voice full of suppressed excitement.

"The kid's been spotted landing on Lanai. Helicopter's on its way to take us there."

Chapter 16

Ken, Lei, Marcella, and Rogers shoehorned into the small seats of the Bell JetRanger, and moments later it took off from the seldom-used helipad of the Kahului Police Station. "Remind me to tell you something about Stevens," she whispered in Marcella's ear. Her friend nodded with a quick frown, but they had to put on their helmets and the roar of the rotors drowned out any conversation.

Lei watched the nondescript houses of the suburbs of Kahului race by at dizzying speed, and soon they were over the waving green of the last of Hawaii's sugarcane fields. Moments later, they were bucking the wind over Ma`alaea Harbor, clocked in as the windiest harbor in the world. Marcella's face had gone a waxy green, and Ken and Rogers both looked stoic, but Lei felt fine as long as she pasted her forehead against the curved window and looked out.

Lanai, a tiny, privately owned island, was sixteen miles off the coast of Lahaina. It been used for pineapple growing, but now was owned by a computer billionaire and was dedicated to a small, exclusive tourist trade. The helicopter flew low over the cerulean water, arrow-straight toward the island, and Lei looked for whales as she thought over what they knew about the Bandit's latest move.

The Bandit had been spotted taking off from Kaanapali, the sighting called in by a citizen who'd seen the shiny chrome-colored craft heading across the wind-whipped channel toward Lanai. Lei wondered what the target on Lanai was; a quick workup on the island and geomaps had produced a likely area of landing in the golf course, in an area fronted by huge and exclusive homes. Ang was busy working up a list of likely addresses.

What could the Smiley Bandit's endgame be, that he was taking these kinds of chances with open-water crossings? Marcella had shown her a newsfeed on her phone that the Bandit had sent to the media, and the distorted, backlit figure of the Bandit's accomplice intoned, "The one percent can't hide anymore. The Smiley Bandit is taking his life in his hands and going to the 'exclusive island' to redistribute more wealth."

Lei found she could hardly stand watching Wendy Watanabe's smug face as the reporter added her commentary. The gag order still hadn't come in, and Ken's terse shake of the head when she asked about it wasn't encouraging.

She had a bad feeling about how this was going to end, even with the pile of rifles between the seats loaded with rubber ammo—the kid had a gun with real bullets. And there were a lot of cops involved who might not have really read the memo about no deadly force…or taken it seriously if they had. The little speech Stevens had made in the station about neutralizing the threat came to mind—and there was something suicidal in the way the kid kept pushing forward.

She wished she could talk to her ex-therapist Dr. Wilson about it. She reached up and tapped her comm unit, built into the helmet. "What do you guys think of a consult with Dr. Wilson about the kid's state of mind?"

"Good idea," Marcella said. "I'm a little worried about the pace of these robberies, what targets he's picking and why. Not to mention that Walther pistol he's packing."

"I'll set it up." Rogers worked his phone. The tinny tone of their voices barely registered over the roar of the helicopter's engines, now laboring as the aircraft bucked against a backswirl off of the golden red, humped shape of Lanai.

Lei focused on the steep, rocky face of the cliff overlooking a small, horseshoe-shaped bay filled with boats as they approached Manele Harbor. Everything from catamarans to fishing boats jammed the narrow docking area, and the helicopter swung alarmingly as it hit some sort of air current. Marcella heaved into her airsick bag, but Rogers and Ken, though clutching theirs, appeared to be holding off for the moment.

Lei was delighted by her first glimpse of the wild, wind-scored island as they rose with the terrain, heading inland and tracking a back-switching paved road that led up from the harbor to the tiny town at the crest of the island.

"Lanai City," the pilot said into their comm units. The "city" was a village square enclosed by small, plantation-style homes left over from the pineapple days. The mansions were a newer development on the outskirts.

"We're landing outside of town and local PD is meeting us to drive out to the unsub's likely targets," Ken said. "So far, no one has spotted the Hummel."

"Are you sure it even went here, then?" Lei asked.

"No. He could have gone farther south and headed for Molokai." The three islands, clustered close, were separated by around nine miles of open ocean. "We've called MPD out there to send patrols to look for the aircraft."

Lei took in the surrounding topography—Lanai was a dry island except for the ridgeline of its highest point, dotted by tall Cook pines that wicked moisture down and captured clouds to cover the little town. Another single two-lane road led from the "city" to the industrial harbor on another side of the island from the bluff they'd arrived on.

The helicopter began descending with more alarming pendulum swinging and landed in the emerald-green grass of a sweep of golf course. Through the curved glass, Lei could see a row of mansions, windows glittering like fool's gold.

She was the last to get out, running a little bent beneath the slowing rotors, carrying a pair of shotguns loaded with beanies. They'd brought several extras in case local law enforcement didn't have theirs ready.

That law enforcement, a sheriff and a pair of deputies, pushed away from their Maui Police Department blue-and-white Crown Vics to greet Ken and Rogers. Marcella, still a little green, refrained from shaking hands with Sheriff Beck and Officers Eno and Mikado.

"Here are some rifles already loaded with beanies," Rogers said. "We have a lot of media attention and child advocates watching this, so if we have a chance to take this kid down, use these."

"What's the kid carrying?" Eno asked. He was an older local guy with acne scars and a bristling mustache that reminded Lei of her ex-partner, Pono.

"Walther PPK, six rounds in the chamber, no other ammo that we know of. Everyone should be in vests," Rogers said.

"Hell, if that kid fires on us, we're going to do what we need to do," Sheriff Beck said, even as he took the rifle with its non-deadly ammo.

"We get it," Marcella said, "but I don't think you quite realize what a media shitstorm this has become."

"The Smiley Bandit has his own Facebook fan page." Lei handed the extra rifle she carried to Officer Mikado, a slender young Japanese man with the wiry, chiseled look of a martial artist. "And he's getting national coverage. We have to take him alive."

They'd brought three vehicles, and Lei ended up in one with Mikado. They pulled out without sirens or lights. "I think the others have it covered here at the McMansion Strip," Mikado said. "I'd like to go out and look somewhere off the beaten track—there's a ripe target at the end of it."

"You know this island," Lei said. "If you think there's another target he'd pick, let's go. We're waiting on a list of targets from our IT agent, but she hasn't gotten back to us yet."

The young officer needed no further encouragement, and they roared out of the area, streaking through the quiet streets of the village with its pickup trucks and colorful tin-roofed cottages built in the pineapple days.

They passed the gracious Koele Lodge with its huge banyans and circle drive surrounded by more Cook and Norfolk pines and continued on the blacktop to an unmarked turnoff. Lei clutched the dashboard as he took the turn hard and accelerated up what must be an entrance to yet another opulent estate—this one bordered with beds planted three feet deep in pineapple, the purplish bromeliad that had covered the island in its agricultural heyday.

Once again a black steel gate barred their path, but this time Mikado punched a code he had memorized into the plinth and the gate swung inward. They roared forward.

The house ahead was more breathtaking than anything Lei had yet seen. Built as a medieval castle of imported golden stone, it stood in turreted glory behind a round rose garden speared by an American flag.

"Let me guess. The big boss's place," Lei said.

"Yes. This is usually Lanai's owner's house. The computer guy hasn't moved in yet, but we expect him any day."

Lei got out of the police vehicle just as one side of the huge, iron-banded oak front door opened. A maid in a traditional black costume with an apron stood there, looking like a bit player in a period piece with her upswept hair topped by a lacy cap—but her eyes were wide with distress and her finger trembling as she pointed to the right side of the castle. "Thank God you came! Hurry, we've been robbed!"

That was all Lei needed to dive back into the vehicle, grab the shotgun, and toss the other one to Mikado. "Don't follow me until you get your vest on," she said to the young officer, who flushed as he popped the trunk of the vehicle.

Lei nodded to the maid and took off in the direction she'd pointed. She hurried at a jog along a crushed-shell walkway that fronted beds of roses planted up against the golden stone. She tightened down the Kevlar and crouched to minimize herself as a target as she came around the corner of the castle—only to hear a now-familiar sound, the high-pitched sewing-machine whine of the Hummel's engine powering up.

It was parked about a hundred yards away from her on what must be a croquet field, because as Lei ran forward, she tripped on a wire wicket and almost went down. She felt Mikado grab the back of her vest to keep her from falling. He must have run full blast to catch up with her.

"Thanks," she said. "It's firing up. Let's get in front of it and block his escape."

They ran toward the Hummel even as it moved forward, bumping over the grass, and Lei could see it was off-kilter—one of the struts was bent, and that tilted the wings off-center.

Lei poured on some speed. The Bandit couldn't shoot at them with the plastic hood down; they just needed to physically block the ultralight to get him to stop. She could see the shadow of a head inside that shiny, round, clear carapace, and she ran as hard as she could—but the Hummel was accelerating at the same speed.

Mikado passed her, running full on, and he had his rifle up. The young officer had game—he must be in good shape to pass her—and maybe Mikado could reach the Hummel in time. Lei stopped and knelt in firing position. She cocked the rifle and aimed a beanie round at the plastic dome of the little aircraft.

The rifle blast was loud, so loud she couldn't hear the sewing-machine drone anymore, and the kick of the recoil knocked her shoulder back. The round hit the dome but did no damage. She fired another round, this time at one of the tires. It made the little plane wobble, but it kept going, bouncing as it tried to take off from the grass.

Mikado was running with all his heart and soul, but it didn't look like he was going to catch up as the ultralight continued to accelerate, its bounces into the air higher each time.

Time to try something heavier. Stopping that aircraft might be her last chance to save the kid. Lei pulled her Glock and aimed at the tail fin. She steadied, lined up her sights, and fired. Even with the crack of the report, she heard a *ping* and saw a fist-sized hole appear in the shiny metal of the tail, and its rudderlike movement stopped.

But the Hummel kept going.

She caught up with Mikado and they watched as the damaged ultralight lifted awkwardly into the air, wobbling and tipping to the side.

"Shit." Lei's stomach churned. She holstered her weapon. This couldn't end well. Her attempt to disable the craft had crippled it just enough to make flying even more hazardous.

They watched the bumpy ascension of the Hummel. It curved at first, as if following the road—and then it straightened off, still flying low. Lei saw a little smoke coming from the propeller—maybe it had been damaged more than she'd thought. Lei speed-dialed Ken and briefed him as they watched the struggling craft. "I shot the tail with a live round and hit him elsewhere with some beanies. He's got to come down soon."

"Get some four-wheel drives," Mikado said. "We should be able to catch him in the open land outside of town. He has to bring it down."

Lei was relaying that when the little plane veered again—and this time, it headed straight for the ocean.

"He's making a run for Molokai! That plane is damaged. He'll never make it!" Lei exclaimed.

"Meet us back at the helipad. I'll alert the MPD over on Molokai," Ken said. "And the Coast Guard."

Lei and Mikado jogged back to the cruiser and waved at the maid. "Someone will be back to take a statement on what's missing," Lei called to her. They put on the siren and lights and headed for the helipad area.

"Do you think he'll make it?" Mikado asked. His brows were knit above his strong nose, lips pursed.

"No telling. I can't believe he'd go for it. I thought I'd ground him for sure." Lei felt terrible. That kid was going down. There was no way the Hummel, already off-kilter with a bent strut, was going to make it across the turbulent, gusty nine-mile Kalohi Channel to Molokai.

Her bullet might be what sent him into the ocean. Still, if it hadn't been that, it would have been something else, she told herself. She wished they'd had time to do the consult with Dr. Wilson, but something inside her knew the truth—the Smiley Bandit had always meant this to be a one-way trip.

The cruiser pulled up at the open area where the JetRanger waited, ready for liftoff.

"I can direct us to where he headed out," Lei said as the three other agents climbed in and everyone put on their flight helmets. With a brief wave to her new friend Mikado, Lei pointed through the rounded Plexiglas. "Straight ahead."

Chapter 17

The helicopter took mere minutes to orient on the golden-stoned castle and draw a bead on the weaving trajectory the Hummel had taken. The pilot pushed forward the collective to top speed, and they zoomed down the arid sculptured flank of Lanai toward the deep cobalt of the surging channel between the islands.

"You say you hit the tail fin?" Marcella asked through the comm unit.

"Yeah. Used my Glock, since the beanies weren't doing anything." Lei's stomach was still knotted, and it wasn't just the turbulence that filled her with a hollow dread.

"That could come back to bite us," Ken said.

Lei turned from her front seat to glare at her partner. "I wanted to disable the aircraft. The beanies weren't doing that. The Hummel was already damaged. One of the struts was bent, and I hit the Plexi cover with a beanie round. He still didn't stop. I hit one of the tires, and again the beanie didn't do a thing. But one bullet from a nine mil stopped that tail rudder cold, and it was exactly what I aimed at. Any sensible unsub would maybe fly a little way and then land, try to get away on foot. But I'm thinking this kid has a death wish and has had it from the beginning. All this is just a setup for the inevitable, rubber ammo or no. We're being used to make a statement."

"It's possible," Ken replied. "I did get ahold of our psychologist, Dr. LaSota, but she's still at Quantico for something so she cleared us to use Dr. Wilson, who's reviewing the case with Ang on Oahu. I hope she'll have some feedback for us on the unsub soon."

The helicopter buzzed over the churning, wind-whipped sea. Lei scanned the ocean in front of them with field glasses and Rogers did so from the side window, while Ken and Marcella worked phones with the Coast Guard and Molokai Police Department respectively. Lei reached to the side to loosen her vest, and her hand slid into her pocket to rub the white-gold disc she still carried.

Stevens. He was lost to her now, but he'd loved her well as long as she'd let him. And he

was giving her back her dog. Somehow, these background thoughts comforted her in the midst of the stressful chase in a bumpy helicopter over a churning ocean.

The wind caught the JetRanger, giving it an alarming dip and heave—and she thought she spotted something, a gleam that wasn't the right color for foam on the waves.

"There!" Lei cried, pointing. "I think I see it!"

The pilot tilted the collective in the direction she pointed, and Ken said, "Coast Guard's on the move, but I don't know how fast they can get here from Kaunakakai Harbor on Molokai."

Lei found herself leaning forward to almost touch the instrument panel, but the four-point harness held her back. They overtook the Hummel rapidly, and Lei's heart sank as she visually measured the distance between the craft, weaving about five hundred feet above the water, and the coast of Molokai. She put her field glasses up and could see smoke trailing from the propeller. The bobbing, weaving flight path resembled that of a drunken pelican.

She put the glasses up to scan the coast—the terrain was a

savannahlike open field of dry grasses, ending with rocky beach. If he could just make it to land, bringing the ultralight down looked relatively easy.

They circled the straining little aircraft.

"What do you want to do?" the pilot asked. "We can open the doors, if you want to bring it down."

"Waxman's given direction—we're to track the aircraft and rescue the Bandit if he's in trouble and apprehend him when he lands," Marcella said.

"I hope we have enough fuel to keep this up," the pilot said. "We're low. I didn't have time to fill up before I picked you up for the trip from Maui, and fighting this wind sucks a lot of fuel."

A new concern. Could this situation get any worse? Lei wondered, and thought it probably could.

The coast of Molokai approached with agonizing slowness. The pilot, conserving his fuel, throttled back to fly alongside the struggling ultralight, and Lei put her field glasses to her eyes, looking over at the shadowed figure inside the clear Plexiglas bubble.

That dark head turned, and a face looked at her—a small face, pale with terror and determination. A face with big brown eyes, a straight little nose, and full lips set in a line of defiance.

A teenaged girl's face.

Lei dropped the glasses and they locked eyes. The expression—the narrowed eyes, the tilt of the chin—told Lei that this was a girl who'd do what she set out to do, or die trying. Lei recognized that expression. She'd worn it herself more than once.

And then the girl lifted an elegant, long-fingered hand and flipped Lei the bird.

Chapter 18

They must have all spotted the girl at the same time, because Rogers said, "Aw, shit-damn." His Texas drawl had gone thick, as it did when he was upset.

Marcella speed-dialed Waxman, and Lei could hear her murmuring: "Female suspect, looks like a local" and "Who the hell is this kid? Do we even have a girl in the suspect pool?"

Lei remained spellbound, watching the lurching, weaving craft and the girl's tense face focused on the shore. If the plane went down, it was likely her bullet that had done it, and the knowledge made her hands sweat. With the field glasses, Lei could see the pointy profile of Angel, Max Smiley's teacup Chihuahua, tucked into the neck of the girl's shirt.

The Smiley Bandit was a teenaged girl. It was more than a PR nightmare; it was the stuff of legend.

Ken's voice in her ear roused her as if from a trance.

"Looks like the ultralight's going down." Indeed, the craft had sunk another twenty feet, lower than they could keep pace with in the helicopter.

"She doesn't want to kill the dog. She's going to try to get to shore to save it, then get us to take her down. I bet she fires on us." Lei couldn't explain the total conviction she had about the girl's state of mind.

"How do you know?" Marcella argued.

"I just know she's going to try to suicide. This was always a one-way trip for this kid."

"Well, we won't let her," Rogers said. "We'll find some other way."

"C'mon, come on, come on," Lei found herself chanting under her breath as they tracked the aircraft's descent, now within a couple hundred yards of the rocky shore—but it was a couple hundred yards too far.

The little plane dipped and bobbled, and the damaged wing caught the water, spiraling the Hummel around. Spray shot up and hit the windshield, and the helicopter, tracking, veered up and away from a flurry of splash as the ultralight spun, tumbled, and plowed nose-first into the water.

It had gone down only a couple hundred yards from the rocky shore, but the sea was still a deep cobalt blue.

"We have to help her!" Lei reached over and hit the door opener, and the side of the JetRanger shot open.

"Coast Guard's on the way," Ken said, and indeed they could see a cutter in the distance—but Lei could also see that the little aircraft, while it had landed upright and seemed miraculously undamaged, was sinking.

The Plexi top flipped open, and the girl pulled herself up to standing even as the front of the Hummel made a sudden lurching dive nose-first. Water poured into the little craft.

"Get closer!" Lei screamed. The helicopter lowered. "Let's throw her a rope or something!"

The girl unzipped her jacket and took out the little dog. She pitched the Chihuahua into the waves, pointing the animal toward shore.

Then, even as the water swirled up around her knees, she pulled the Walther and aimed at the helicopter. She pulled the trigger, and the report knocked her backward. Lei heard the *ping* of a bullet hitting metal. The pilot spun the craft away, even as Marcella and Rogers, in a better position near the door, cocked their rifles and took aim at the defiant figure.

Lei spotted the little dog, confused, swimming back toward the sinking aircraft.

"Angel!" Lei cried. "She's turned around!" She opened the small cockpit side door, flung off her helmet and harness, ignoring the cries of the pilot and her fellow agents.

Lei felt the force of her will connecting with that of the girl as she pointed to the dog in the water, catching the girl's eye. She was fully exposed to the Bandit's gunfire, a ripe target—and somehow she knew the kid wouldn't take the shot. The Bandit seemed to have heard Lei's frantic message, and the girl turned away from the helicopter, scanning the water. She spotted the dog's tiny head, struggling in the surging waves and about to be sucked down.

"What're you doing?" Marcella yelled, even as Lei crouched in the door of the helicopter, holding on to the door frame. The Bandit flung the pistol away and dove away from the doomed ultralight, swimming toward Angel, but Lei could see she wouldn't reach the animal in time—the tiny dog's head disappeared under the waves even as the Hummel gurgled it's last moments.

Lei pumped her lungs full of air and jumped out of the helicopter, aiming as best she could for where she'd last seen the Chihuahua. She lost sight of that spot on the water as she flew through the air, keeping her arms tight against her sides and feet together—but the water still felt like concrete as she hit, the shock of it slamming from the soles of her feet to the top of her head, buckling her knees and stealing her breath.

Lei opened her arms, kicking and swimming toward the surface, opening her eyes underwater. The salt water stung, and it was blurry—but she thought she saw a dark blotch straight ahead. She kicked hard, swimming toward it, her now-empty lungs screaming for air.

Lei scooped the Chihuahua into her arms and powered up through the water with her legs. Even weighted by the Kevlar vest, clothes, and athletic shoes, she was in shape, a strong swimmer, and she bore the dog to the surface, thrusting them both into air with a giant gasp. A wave promptly smacked her in the face as she treaded water, the Kevlar vest filling and weighting her down, her shoes heavy as iron.

Angel wasn't moving.

The girl splashed over to reach her, dark eyes frantic. "Is she alive?"

"Take her," Lei choked, thrusting the tiny dog into the girl's hands. "Swim hard for shore."

Without another word, the girl struck out for shore, holding Angel up above the waves with one hand.

Lei could see the helicopter still circling overhead, but her attention was now fully occupied with staying afloat. She was in trouble, weighted by the vest, her firearm, and accoutrements. She leaned over underwater and pulled off her shoes. That helped her kick, and she swam awkwardly after the Bandit, sinking a little lower with each stroke. Lei shed the Kevlar next, not sad to see the hated vest spiral into the depths. She was pretty sure she could make it now, her eyes on the seal-dark head of the girl swimming in front of her.

Lei staggered up into the shallows behind the Bandit, bare feet scraped by the rocky bottom, her legs rubbery, lungs burning, and eyes stinging with salt. The girl turned to her, and the little dog, cradled in her arms, still wasn't moving.

"Help her!" the Bandit cried, face white and dark eyes wide.

Chapter 19

*T*urn her upside down," Lei said. "Let's try giving her chest compressions." Surely the basics for drowning used on a human would be the same for a dog. She was dimly aware of the helicopter spiraling down to land on the slope behind them.

The Bandit upended the Chihuahua by her hind legs and held her against her body as Lei pried open the dog's jaws, pushing the tongue out of the way with one finger as she compressed the dog's side with the other. Foamy water pumped out of the dog's mouth.

Lei kept going, compressing the lungs manually with one hand and holding the tongue out of the way with the other until suddenly the tiny body jerked. Angel thrashed and vomited water over Lei as she knelt on the rocks.

"Oh, thank God!" the girl exclaimed, hugging the tiny dog. "And thank *you*," she said to Lei.

"You're welcome," Lei said, grinning. "Thank God is right." The tiny Chihuahua twisted around to lick the Bandit's face just as Ken arrived, cuffs in hand.

"You're under arrest," he said. "Put your hands behind your back."

"Take care of Angel," the Smiley Bandit said, and handed the tiny, shivering Chihuahua to Lei.

"I will." Lei hated the defeat in the girl's eyes, the way they slid away as she turned around and put her hands behind her back. Ken moved in and cuffed her, leading her up the rocks onto the rocky red dirt of Molokai.

Kaunakakai Police Station was a rustic building in the middle of a Western-themed town dressed in the false fronts and bright paint of that style. Wrapped in a striped beach towel, handcuffed, and seated at a battered interview table, the Smiley Bandit looked even more unlikely than she had when Lei had first spotted her.

The other agents, seemingly unanimously, let Lei be the first to interview her. Lei set a portable video camera on the table, pointed in the girl's direction

"I'm Special Agent Lei Texeira with the FBI. What's your name?" Lei's clothes were still soaked with ocean water, as were the girl's, but Lei held the tiny, trembling Chihuahua on her lap, and the girl's dark eyes were on the dog as she answered.

"Consuelo Aguilar."

"And…How did this happen? All this?" Lei knew she should ask better questions, but she found herself tongue-tied, unsure how to start.

"It's a long story." The heavy metal handcuff looked obscene on the delicately fashioned wrist that Consuelo reached toward the dog. Angel whined and wriggled, straining toward the girl, and Lei finally set the tiny dog on the table. The Chihuahua trotted over and jumped into Consuelo's lap.

Lei's earbud crackled. "Running her. No priors, aged sixteen, attended McKinley High until she dropped out this year. Work fast. Wendy Watanabe's on the way, and she's organized a fund to hire Bennie Fernandez. He's sending representation."

Lei cursed inwardly, but a larger part of her was relieved. Consuelo would have the best defense lawyer in Hawaii. Bennie

Fernandez was a cherubic little man with a Santa-like beard who wooed juries. He had been a thorn in Marcella's side in several cases in the past.

"I'll let you hold the dog, but you have to give us a statement."

The girl's long lashes dropped over remarkable dark eyes as she petted the dog in her lap. "It doesn't matter anymore, anyway."

Consuelo's father, Constantino Aguilar, had been an airplane mechanic working for Paradise Air for twenty years. He'd been a stickler for detail and quality, and he'd come down with colon cancer, diagnosed too late. Max Smiley had taken that opportunity to let him go, refusing his application for health-related leave and terminating his employment for absenteeism when the cancer got too bad for him to come to work.

He'd gone home to his sister's house and taken four months to die, during which Consuelo had nursed him.

"And where's your mother?" Lei asked, wondering who the girl's guardian was.

"She died. Hit by a drunk driver," Consuelo said. She petted Angel rather hard, but the tiny dog's eyes just shut in bliss. Lei's earbud crackled, and this time Ang's voice filled her ear. They must be piping her in from Oahu to run background.

"Mother is Victoria Aguilar, killed in vehicular hit-and-run two years ago. Was walking with Consuelo when a drunk driver came up on the curb and ran her down."

Lei sucked in her breath in a little gasp, her mind filling in the details of the horror that fourteen-year-old Consuelo must have gone through.

"Don't feel sorry for me." Consuelo looked up at Lei, and her eyes had gone hard and narrowed. "I knew exactly what I was doing. Max Smiley and the rest of the one percent, people who exploit others—they deserve what they've got coming."

"So you think that chip on your shoulder justifies ripping people off."

"I wasn't ripping people off. I was practicing wealth redistribution."

"Fancy words," Lei said. "You took a shot at federal officers. Who else have you been working with? Who is the guy in the videos?"

The door opened, and a dapper, dark-skinned man in an aloha shirt and chinos entered. "I'm Frank Reza, Consuelo Aguilar's temporary counsel, and she's a minor. Please refrain from any further questions."

Marcella had followed him in. "We can question her, and you can be present," she argued, hands on shapely hips.

"Then at least let the girl get a shower, some food, and change into dry clothes. This is not humane treatment, and she's a child."

"Some child! We have a right to question this fugitive until we're satisfied we know at least the extent of her plot and network and that it's been disabled," Marcella said.

"Network! Plot! You make the girl sound like a terrorist," Reza said indignantly. Only Lei saw the way the girl's eyes flared wide at the mention of "terrorist" before she lowered them, focusing on petting the little dog. Reza touched her shoulder, and she looked up at him. "Bennie Fernandez is on his way—I'm his Molokai associate. You're in good hands now."

Lei experienced a shiver of unease as Consuelo slanted a glance over at Lei. "I'm done talking," she said.

And, with Reza planted at her side, it appeared she was. Marcella came in and had a crack at her, and so did Ken and Rogers. Lei finally wrestled the dog out of her arms and went outside the office, hoping that would help get her to talk—but Ken came out a few minutes later, shaking his head. "She won't give up Rezents, where he is, what he's doing, or even if he's her partner."

"We should just check in with Wendy Watanabe; she's probably got better intel," Lei said a little bitterly, setting Angel down in front of a saucer of water a kindly officer had poured. The outer office door opened and Watanabe, bright as a parakeet, walked in trailing her cameraman. "Speak of the devil."

Watanabe spotted Lei and made a beeline across the office to her. "I hear you have the Bandit in custody."

"No comment," Lei said. Ken looked inscrutable beside her, his arms folded.

Watanabe looked down at the tiny Chihuahua, lapping water. "This is Angel, Max Smiley's dog!" She gestured to the cameraman. "Get a shot of it!"

The man hoisted up the camera to his shoulder and zeroed in on Angel, who scuttled up against Lei's soaked black pants, trembling. Lei scooped the dog up and the camera turned on her, Watanabe's microphone appearing in her face. "Agent Texeira, this dog is Angel, the Chihuahua the Smileys have reported missing. What's the status of the Smiley Bandit? We know from Coast Guard transmissions that the Hummel went down close to shore here on Molokai."

"No comment." Lei pushed the microphone away as Angel, terrified, tried to burrow into her neck. Ken turned the reporter by force and pushed her and the cameraman toward the door, gesturing with his head to a couple of officers, who assisted.

"This is a police station and this is an active investigation. Get outside." They forcibly put the intrepid reporter outside the building, the cameraman recording the whole thing.

Lei could hear Watanabe monologuing on the steps. Adrenaline aftermath from the chase was setting in, and Lei sat abruptly on one of the metal chairs as Ken returned. "Did you ever line up Dr. Wilson? Because I think we should do a psych eval on Consuelo. I have a bad feeling about what's going on with her."

"Yeah, soon as we transport her. We'll take the helicopter back to Oahu and get that rolling."

Marcella stuck her head out of the interview room. "We're

done here for now. Let's get her on the chopper and into a holding cell. We can have another go tomorrow."

Reza followed her out. "I'll ride with her on the helicopter."

"No, you won't. The chopper is not rated for civilian transport." Marcella's voice was crisp. "You can arrange for representation to meet us at the helipad. I'm sure Bennie can work it into his schedule."

Rogers led Consuelo out by the elbow, looking impossibly young and small in a set of borrowed sweats. "Pilot says the chopper is refueled and ready to go."

Ken ended up staying behind on Molokai to wait for a civilian flight out and oversee the retrieval of the Hummel. It was being hauled in by the Coast Guard, and Ken was to take possession of whatever Consuelo had stolen from the stone castle on Lanai.

Lei climbed into the helicopter last, carrying Angel. Consuelo sat in the farthest seat back from the pilot against the side window. Marcella and Rogers had left the seat beside her open for Lei, and she took it, checking the girl's four-point seat belt and setting a protective helmet on her head, adjusting the strap under her chin.

Consuelo's head lolled apathetically, and even Angel's excited licks failed to rouse the girl.

The chopper lifted, weaving a little in the wind, and after climbing, drew a line for Oahu.

"I think something's wrong with her." Lei's forehead knit as she spoke into the comm. Consuelo's eyes fluttered, and she flopped forward, held upright only by the harness.

"She's probably faking. Don't let her out of the restraints," Marcella said. Lei didn't think the girl could fake the waxy color of her normally olive-brown complexion, but maybe she'd just collapsed from the stress of the chase. They'd given her water, but Lei wondered when she'd last eaten.

Lei palmed one of the thin little wrists. The girl's pulse was fast and uneven, her eyes closed and face pale. "Do you have any water? I think she's fainted."

Rogers, ever prepared, took a metal canteen out of his backpack and handed it to her. Lei tried to push Consuelo's lolling head upright.

"Wake up, Consuelo. Water." She tried to pour the water into the girl's mouth, and it dribbled back out. She looked in alarm at Marcella. "Call ahead. Have Dr. Wilson meet us with an ambulance. Something's wrong with her."

"Don't unstrap her!" Marcella barked, but Lei did anyway, hitting the buckle that autoreleased the four-point harness. Marcella locked the release button on the side door, but she needn't have bothered.

Consuelo fell out of her seat to fold into the narrow space in front in a fetal position.

Lei pulled the girl's unresponsive body into her arms and held her as Rogers took out the medical kit and checked her vitals. Marcella worked the phone lining up the emergency medical services.

The flight to Oahu felt endless as Lei held the slight girl in her arms. She found out later it had been only forty minutes. She stroked the dark hair back from Consuelo's forehead while Angel burrowed into the girl's side, whimpering.

"She's unconscious but breathing is good. Blood pressure very low," Rogers said. "She's probably just in shock."

The emergency medical technicians and Dr. Wilson, blond bob dancing in the wind from the rotors, met them at the FBI rooftop helipad. Lei found herself reluctant to let go of Consuelo as the EMTs and Dr. Wilson climbed into the helicopter to take over. Angel began high-pitched, hysterical barking and grabbed on to the navy blue pant leg of one of the EMTs. Lei caught the little dog and climbed out of the helicopter, her eyes on the still figure now wrapped in a blanket with an IV in her hand.

"Lei." Marcella put a hand on her arm, her warm brown eyes concerned. "She's getting help. Dr. Wilson will assess her. We'll make sure she's cuffed to the hospital bed and not going anywhere."

Lei held the dog close, watching as they moved Consuelo onto a gurney and covered her with a tucked-in white sheet that made her skin look sallow. The girl was so thin, she barely lifted the sheet. Only her long, shiny black hair, freed from the knot she'd tied it in and fluttering off the edge of the gurney, looked alive.

"She's dehydrated and in shock," one of the paramedics said, taking his stethoscope out of his ears. Dr. Wilson's lips pursed.

"Doesn't explain why she's unconscious," the psychologist said. "I'd better ride along. I'd like to admit her to the adolescent psych unit at Tripler for suicide watch."

"Thanks, Dr. Wilson." Lei smiled gratefully at her former therapist. "I'm worried she's trying to check out on life since the attempt at 'suicide by cop' failed. I don't think she wants to live anymore."

"Yes. Marcella told me what you were concerned about." Keen blue eyes that had always been able to see into Lei's soul swept her with their searchlight. "I think you'd better go get some rest, too, and a little detachment from this case."

"Okay." Lei clutched the dog tighter as she turned back to Marcella and Rogers. "What's the plan?"

"Go home, Lei. Get a hot shower and a change of clothes. We'll all do the same," Marcella said. "Consuelo's secure, but we still need to locate Rezents and Blackman—hopefully this Bandit thing was all her idea and there won't be any further activity now that she's in custody, but who knows? Waxman has us briefing at oh-six hundred tomorrow morning."

"What about the dog?" Lei asked.

"Seems like you've got the suspect in custody," Marcella said, with one of those vibrant dimpled smiles. "Report in tomorrow, and I'll call you if anything develops."

Lei gave her friend a brief hug. "Thanks. This one got to me."

"I don't think anyone's going to forget the Smiley Bandit anytime soon—this girl got to all of us. You said you were going to tell me something about Stevens?"

"It can wait." Lei had forgotten all about her encounter with Stevens in the drama of the day. Memory brought familiar pain, but she hoped it was a tiny bit less than this morning.

"Okay. Well, now we just need to round up whoever's left and figure out what's been going on. Thank God we brought her in safely—though you about gave me a heart attack jumping out of the helicopter." Marcella put her hands on her hips. "That was not part of the plan. It was at least fifty feet! You could easily have drowned!"

"She would have, for sure, if I hadn't jumped." Lei stroked the domed head of the Chihuahua, who had gone limp with tiredness and attention. "But I bet Waxman won't like it."

"He's not the only one." Rogers said as he returned. "Get home and get cleaned up and some rest. I've no doubt Waxman's going to take some chunks out of your hide tomorrow morning—you'll need your game face on."

"I'm sorry. I had to do what I had to do." This conversation reminded Lei of a dozen she'd had with Stevens, but this time she felt real regret for the worry she'd caused her friends.

They watched the EMTs pushing Consuelo's gurney and Dr. Wilson go into the building, heading for the ambulance just as Bennie Fernandez, his cherubic Santa profile all a-jiggle with unaccustomed speed, arrived. Her last glimpse of Consuelo was the black silk of the girl's hair trailing in the breeze as the group got onto the transport elevator, followed by Fernandez and Marcella, who'd charged onto the elevator at the last minute to intercept Fernandez.

Consuelo would be safe at Tripler, under medical supervision. It was all over but the cleanup—or so Lei hoped.

Chapter 20

*L*ei made her way to her truck in the lowest level of the parking garage, her shoes squishing and pant legs rubbing, the exhausted little dog asleep in the crook of her arm. The shoes and pants reminded her of another investigation she'd never forget—the drowning of two young girls back in Hilo. The feeling of the wet black silk of Haunani Pohakoa's hair in her hands as she towed the drowned girl out of the pond where they'd washed up would always haunt her. Haunani was a girl she'd known and felt a connection to—and been too late to help.

She felt that connection even more for brave Consuelo Aguilar. Lei couldn't explain how she knew what the girl was thinking and feeling—there was just something there, a kinship.

At her building, she stopped to let Angel sniff and piddle in the grass in front of the shower tree. The three flights of stairs had never felt so long, the light dimming as she trudged higher to her floor and unlocked the door.

She set Angel down on the floor to explore her new quarters

and went to do her own perimeter check—all windows and doors were secure, and the apartment had a dusty, closed-up smell she hoped would blow out as she opened the sliders.

"Taking a shower, Angel," she told the little dog. "Let's go get that salt water off you."

She washed the little dog, wriggling and snorting, in the bathroom sink. The Chihuahua, so much tinier than Keiki but with the same black and tan points, reminded Lei of her dog. She needed to hurry up and work on finding a new, dog-friendly place where Keiki could be at home. She hopped into the shower, and the hot water caressing her body felt heavenly, cleansing away the sweat and salt of another busy day in the FBI.

Angel was waiting on the bath mat outside the shower, and Lei thought regretfully of how she had to call Max Smiley and return the little dog to him—but after hearing Consuelo's story, she was even less inclined to hurry.

Lei had never seen the appeal of these kinds of dogs until now, but when she climbed into her inflatable mattress that night with Angel in the crook of her arm, the comfort the little Chihuahua brought was undeniable.

Her mind drifted back over the case, imagining young Consuelo Aguilar, fueled by idealistic rage, flying that ridiculous plane into those ridiculous situations, Angel her only comfort. And a comfort she must have been.

But where were her accomplices? Were they even Rezents and Blackman? It seemed like a good assumption, but Consuelo herself had turned the whole investigation on its ear. And the Kwon murder remained a constant thread of anxiety that ran through the back of her thoughts. Lei was glad she'd made that difficult call to her grandfather earlier, and it seemed there was no way he could have had anything to do with the shooting—her father was way off base there. But at least Lei had made contact, and they'd meet next week at a noodle house. She found herself smiling a little, wrapped around the tiny dog.

Her sleep was dreamless for once.

Early morning turned the Kaneohe air blue gray as Lei pulled up at the barred automatic gate in front of the Smiley estate. She'd decided to run the dog out to the older couple before the morning briefing, rather than leave her in the apartment where the Chihuahua had begun immediate panic-stricken yapping when Lei tried to leave.

Lei pushed the button on the gate alarm several times and finally heard Max Smiley's gruff voice, rendered tinny by the speaker. "Whaddaya want? Who is this?"

"Special Agent Lei Texeira. Delivery related to your case."

Typical of Max Smiley's style, he didn't respond or thank her, but the black bars motored inward. She drove her Tacoma in and pulled up in front of the entrance, a spread of double doors marked by five-foot bronze Chinese dragon sculptures.

Max opened the door clad in striped terry cloth. His wife, Emmeline, was behind him, and she gave a cry of delight, running forward to snatch Angel out of Lei's arms. "Oh my God! My sweetheart! Angel!"

The little dog appeared equally delighted, whimpering and wriggling, licking Emmeline.

"Thank you! Thank you!" the older woman cried, throwing a free arm around Lei in a hug.

Max's face, a-bristle with white whiskers, had split down the middle with a wide grin. "Come in! Have some coffee. Thanks so much for bringing our Angel back!"

"I can only stay a minute," Lei said. "Got a briefing back in town." She followed the couple, still emitting cries of delight, into the now-familiar kitchen. Max splashed a cup of coffee into a travel mug emblazoned with Paradise Air. "Cream? Sugar?"

"Cream, please."

Smiley dosed it liberally with half-and-half. "Keep the mug," he said, handing it to her. "This must mean you have the Bandit in custody."

"We do. And I wanted to speak to you about that. Unofficially. Off the record."

Emmeline drew close to her husband, placing a hand on his shoulder. "He must have been very disturbed to do all he did."

"Yes. I'm giving you a little heads-up on all that's coming." Lei took a breath, knowing what a chance she was taking saying anything at all about the investigation—but she was thinking of all the unhappy employees at Paradise Air. It was a chance worth taking. "The Smiley Bandit is a girl. The sixteen-year-old daughter of one of your oldest employees, who's deceased now. Constantino Aguilar."

Lei could see by the blood draining from Max Smiley's florid face that he knew exactly who Constantino Aguilar was. Emmeline turned to him, the dog clutched her to pin-tucked breast. "Max! What did you do to that poor man! Constantino was a good employee, the best!"

"It's what your husband didn't do that led to what Consuelo did," Lei said. "Constantino was diagnosed with cancer too late for effective treatment. Your husband wouldn't grant his medical leave and fired him for job abandonment when he became too sick to come to work. He lost his health insurance and his pension. He died at his sister's house, with Consuelo dropping out of school to nurse him. She's an orphan and penniless. And currently in the psych ward at Tripler Hospital on suicide watch."

"Max." Emmeline moved away from her husband. "I can't believe this. You aren't pressing charges on that poor girl."

"I didn't think." Max's face had gone gray, and Lei was a little alarmed as he folded and sat abruptly in a kitchen chair. "I didn't think about anything but the bottom line, and Constantino was always nit-picking, trying to spend more in the engine-maintenance department. I didn't know what was happening to him." He turned to Lei. "I count on Reynalda Tamayose, my personnel manager, to run day-to-day operations. I knew we let him go, but I didn't know he was sick." He shook his head, looked at Emmeline. "I'm sorry, honey. I'm going to make it up to them. Been doing a lot of thinking since the Hummel disappeared."

"I heard rumors about how you were running the company, but I didn't want to believe it. Not you, not my Max. That wasn't how we started the company. We were a family in the early days. I never should have left you alone with it all." She turned back to Lei, blue eyes showing steely resolve, Angel tucked under her arm. "He'll make it right for that girl. Full pension benefits for her to inherit, to begin with. And we won't press charges on the theft."

"It's gone way beyond that now." Lei shook her head. "Consuelo Aguilar is in a world of trouble—but she has a very good lawyer. That reporter Wendy Watanabe started a defense fund for her. The first priority is that she gets some mental health help, which is underway. Anyway, Mr. Smiley, I hope you and your wife will talk things over and consider some policy changes. In our investigation, it became evident your company is more troubled than you know. Much more than it appears on paper."

"I'm sorry it took this situation to give me a wake-up call. I'll call a management team meeting right away."

"And I'll be there, too," Emmeline said. "Thanks again for bringing Angel back safely."

Lei thought of Consuelo tossing away the pistol and diving into the ocean to save the little dog—giving up her chance at death so Angel could live. She vividly remembered the moment she'd caught the little dog underwater and bore her to the surface—and the moment the dog fought her way back to life in Consuelo's arms.

"Do something for Consuelo Aguilar. That's all the thanks I need." Lei reached out to stroke the rounded head, and Angel closed her eyes, her wide bat ears sagging in bliss.

Lei was speeding on the Pali Highway, headed for the Bureau briefing to review the case, when her cell beeped. She put the Bluetooth in and took a call from Ken.

"The Smiley Bandit has struck again," Ken said without greeting. "Get your ass into the office."

Chapter 21

*L*ei slid into one of the padded steel chairs around the Bureau's fake-burled-wood conference table. Ken shot her his you're-late-again glance, but she ignored it, intent on the screen behind Waxman's head—Wendy Watanabe was ahead of them again, in front of a natural-stone mansion this time.

"Kahala residents were shocked this morning to see the graffiti and destruction of this gracious home, owned by pharmaceutical executive Glenn Parry and his wife." The camera panned the stone wall. The edifice of the home was marked with spray-painted graffiti, the distinctive smiley-face signature that Consuelo had left. Smoke belched from the front door, semiobscured by a fire truck. "Inside the home, the Smiley Bandit has apparently struck again, destroying the interior and taking off with several valuable objets d'art. The FBI will not return our calls to comment, but it appears that our initial story, that the Bandit was in custody, was in error."

Lei leaned over to Ken. "Why aren't we out in Kahala with the case?"

"Marcella and Rogers are. Waxman wanted us in here."

Lei's heart lurched. This couldn't be good. Her actions were going to be questioned, and it appeared Waxman wasn't even going to wait until the investigation was over to question them. The video switched to the backlit figure of the Bandit's sidekick.

"You pigs think you brought down the Bandit. Think again. The Smiley Mafia has gone to the streets and it's spreading. Smiley Mafia is the virus that's going to purge the one percent that give nothing back to our islands, to the world. Brace yourselves. The Smiley Mafia will be teaching you some new lessons in wealth redistribution."

Watanabe reappeared, and Lei didn't think she was imagining the real concern that had appeared in the reporter's eyes. "This reporter has never heard the phrase 'Smiley Mafia' until now, and there is a very different tone with this latest video and the attack on the Parry estate, where sources confirm explosives were used. Could this latest attack be a copycat? Or followers of the Bandit seeking revenge? Reporting live from Honolulu, with exclusive coverage of the Smiley Bandit case, this is Wendy Watanabe signing off."

Waxman clicked off the video and looked at Lei. He was immaculate as usual, a subtle red-striped tie setting off a gray summer-weight suit, silver hair gleaming like a helmet and his eyes cold as they surveyed her.

Lei remembered for the first time that she'd dressed in the dark and had failed to do anything to tame the frazzled curls she'd slept on. She glanced down, and sure enough, she'd misbuttoned her shirt. Fortunately, her backup pair of black athletic shoes were on the right feet, and still tied.

She might get fired, but she'd saved Angel's life, and the visit to the Smileys had been successful. Maybe some change for Paradise Air employees would come from it.

"It appears Consuelo Aguilar's accomplices have taken the Smiley Bandit thing in a new direction with Aguilar in custody.

Does anyone know what the hell Smiley Mafia is?" His voice rose on the phrase as he narrowed his eyes at Lei. "Texeira, you look like hell. Not up to Bureau standard; neither have been your actions on this case. If I didn't need you right now, I'd be benching you for that botched interview on Maui, not to mention your pattern of lateness, insubordination, and lack of protocol—such as jumping out of helicopters."

Lei wondered what he'd think of her early-morning trip to see the Smileys and return Angel and decided not to mention it. She resisted the urge to touch her rampageous hair or rebutton her misaligned blouse as he went on. "I'm writing you up, and we'll have a formal administrative conference when this investigation is over. Right now, I need you to get into the psych ward and have a talk with that girl. Marcella, Rogers, and Ken all have told me you have some sort of mystical bond with her. Well, get in there and get me some intel, and if it's good enough, a write-up in your record is all I'll have to do. Find out what the hell the Smiley Mafia is and who her coconspirators are. I don't want to hear from you unless you've got some answers."

"Yes, sir." Lei spoke through numb lips. She stood, scraped back her chair, and walked out, Ken on her heels.

"You're just an inch or two from getting fired. I'm not gonna lie," Ken said. "And it would be a shame, because you're a damn good investigator." He squeezed her shoulder as they walked down the hall. "Hang in there. We'll fight this as we go."

"Don't see what I did that was so terrible," Lei said as they drove in lights-and-sirens glory toward Tripler Hospital, a historic pinkish carbuncle on a hill.

"Like I said, it's a buildup, and also part of Waxman's hazing process with new agents."

"I hear he's harder on women."

"Yeah, I've heard that, too, but I think he'd just say it was your inexperience and attitude. Anyway, I hear Consuelo's better physically, but she hasn't spoken. Dr. Wilson can't get her to engage."

"Great," Lei muttered. "My career's on the line with this interview, and the witness is catatonic."

Consuelo did appear catatonic. She was in a simple room with nothing in it but a toilet in the corner and a built-in cot. No hard corners on anything, anywhere, and the walls were covered with gray carpeting. "Deadens noise, and they can't hurt themselves banging their heads," the sturdy nurse who showed them to Consuelo's room said in reply to Lei's question.

Consuelo lay straight and still on the cot. Her eyes were open as she stared at the ceiling without moving. Her long hair had been confined to a ponytail, and she wore green hospital scrubs with socks on her feet.

Ken took a chair outside, and Lei carried in her phone. She'd taken a picture of Angel the previous evening and printed it out before they came, and she held the picture above Consuelo, where the girl could see it without turning her head.

"Angel says hi." The dog had her huge Chihuahua ears pricked, her round bulgy eyes agleam and her tiny pink tongue hanging out. She really did look like she was saying hi.

A long moment passed, and then Consuelo put her finger out and touched the printout of the dog's face.

"I'm glad you're feeling better." Lei knelt next to the bed, the dearth of furniture bothering her. The space felt more like a prison cell than a hospital room.

Consuelo didn't respond. Lei decided to just ask the questions that needed asking.

"Consuelo, I know you're the real Smiley Bandit. I know you had reasons for what you did. But it looks like, with you in here, Rezents is doing some stuff in your name. We know it's him because we've matched his voice in the videos. He trashed an estate in Kahala. Took a bunch of stuff, vandalized it, graffiti everywhere with your smiley-face logo on it."

Another long moment passed; then Consuelo rolled over and looked at Lei. Her eyes had an expression in them, a vacancy, as if she were coming back from somewhere very far away.

"What?" Her voice was thin and thready.

Lei repeated what she'd said before. "He talked about the Smiley Mafia going viral, going to the streets and redistributing wealth."

A little flare of something alive and angry glittered in the dark of Consuelo's eyes. "Good."

She snatched the photo and rolled away from Lei, tucking the picture of Angel inside her shirt as she faced the wall.

"Consuelo. Talk to me." No response from the girl.

"I took Angel back to the Smileys. I talked to them about your father."

Still no response.

"Consuelo. Please. Tell me who you're working with. We need to bring them in safely."

Still no answer. Lei got up and headed to the door. "Max Smiley said he's sorry. They're giving you back your father's pension."

Consuelo still didn't respond.

Outside in the hall, Dr. Wilson was talking to Ken. "She's been in an almost catatonic state since she got in. I've put her on an antidepressant, hoping to bring her brain chemistry up a bit, but she refuses to eat or take her medication. We're going to give it another day before we start her on a force-feeding regimen."

"I got a response out of her, but it wasn't what we needed." Lei gave the psychologist a brief hug. She described what she'd said and done.

"I wish you'd checked with me first about giving her that information about Rezents," Dr. Wilson said. "Though I think it might take her out of despair to know her 'cause' is continuing. I don't think we can look to her for any help with the investigation, though. Whatever the Smiley Mafia's cause is, she was willing to die for it."

"Was it okay to give her the picture of the dog?" Lei asked. She couldn't seem to do anything right these days.

"That was good. I just wished you'd stopped there."

"Well, what's next for her?"

"We have to stabilize her. Then I guess she can be transferred to the youth correctional center for holding until a bail hearing."

"She's too much of a suicide and flight risk. I hate the thought of her in jail."

"We're on the same page there," Dr. Wilson said. "I'm already prepping an evaluation with recommendations. I want to keep her in a therapeutic setting."

"Hey, sure you two aren't working for Bennie Fernandez?" Ken asked. The lawyer was famous for his bleeding-heart pleas. "The kid's had a rough time, but she still has a boatload of felonies to answer for." Dr. Wilson shook her head. "I think she needs therapy more than anything."

Lei refrained from further comment—an agreement that would further compromise her in Ken's eyes. This kid really had gotten under her skin, and the thought of that slight figure in prison orange turned her stomach. There had to be a way to get her treatment instead. "We need to check in with Marcella and Rogers. I'll call you later, see if she's in a better state to talk."

Lei and Ken got on the road to Kahala, a wealthy neighborhood on the Diamond Head side of the city and the address of the most recent burglary. Lei was silent during the drive through streets bordered by lava-stone walls and gracious plantings. Fit moms pushing jogging strollers and older people with fancy dogs walked opposite them on wide, smooth sidewalks.

The difference between the earlier burglary sites and this one was immediately obvious. Graffiti in harsh red paint began on the exterior of the native bluestone wall and extended into the trashed interior of the house. WEALTH REDISTRIBUTION and BRING DOWN THE 1% NOW along with SMILEY MAFIA were interspersed with the trademark smiley-face design.

Lei put her hands on her hips, gazing around at the destruction—sculptures tipped over off their bases and broken canvases slashed, TVs blown apart by knickknacks. Stuffing spilled out from furniture like intestines from a gut wound. Red spray paint repeated the Smiley Bandit symbol across the walls.

Marcella stepped out of the kitchen. She was immaculately put together—smooth brown hair restrained in the elegant updo she called the FBI Twist, pointy-toed patent slingbacks adding style to black slacks and a plain white blouse. "Lei. Glad you made it over. Did the girl talk at the hospital?"

"No." Lei blew out a breath. "This is really intense, a whole different vibe. Lotta rage here. Think it's a copycat?"

"Copycat or the coconspirators carrying on the mission. What did you make of the Smiley Mafia thing Rezents said on the video this morning? I was watching your interview yesterday. I didn't hear her mention Smiley Mafia."

"No, she never said anything about that. But when I mentioned it today, it got a reaction. She knows what it is; she's just not talking. She hasn't said a word about Rezents or working with anyone else."

"Well, let's hope that changes. Follow me." Marcella led Lei and Ken into the business area of the house and gestured to the office safe. It was a rather cheap residential one, but unlike the others, its door hung open by one hinge, the interior blackened and the desk area splintered. "This Bandit is using explosives."

Chapter 22

Rogers came into the office carrying a camera. "Welcome to the Smiley Bandit's latest crime scene. This kid blew the door off the safe, all right, but from what I can tell, he blew up the money, too." He reached down to pick up a blackened piece of a hundred-dollar bill from the blizzard of bits scattered over the carpet. "Doesn't seem like an expert."

"We haven't been back to the office—has the usual donation thing happened with the stolen goods?" Ken asked.

"Not that we know of. Homeowner says there was about five thousand in there and a collection of Hawaiian gold jewelry, which as you can see, is gone," Rogers said. "He probably took that with him. We haven't found evidence of it."

Marcella drew Lei aside into the hall, leaving Ken and Rogers continuing to investigate. "Waxman sounded pretty pissed off this morning. I don't think he likes how that interview with Watanabe backfired. The 'new face of the FBI' made us look bad. Are you okay?"

"Yeah. I'm getting written up, with an administrative conference when things settle down on the case. He'd like to bench me right now, but he wanted to see if I could get anything out of Consuelo first—which I couldn't." Lei sighed, pushed rioting curls out of her face. "Got a rubber band?"

"No, sorry. So how's Angel doing?"

"I took her out to the Smileys early this morning. It made me late to the briefing, which didn't help. He thinks I'm an insubordinate risk taker with poor communication skills."

Marcella squeezed her shoulder wordlessly. "He hated me, too, for the first six months. You'll get past it. I had a call from Alika Wolcott, asking if you were single, if that's any consolation."

"Oh my God. I can't believe he'd even give me the time of day after the way I treated him on Kaua`i," Lei said. Alika was so attractive, and the idea that he still cared enough to ask about her did give her a little lift. "We'll see. I was going to tell you earlier—I ran into Stevens and Anchara on Maui."

"Oh no!"

"Yeah. I mean, I ran into them literally—I spotted them having breakfast. Stevens had told me he'd let me have Keiki back, which was good news—and that they were having some problems. I admit I let it get my hopes up a little bit—but no." She looked down at the shrapnel of a china vase all around them on the floor. "It's really over. But at least I'll get my dog back."

Marcella pulled Lei's stiff body into her arms for a quick, hard hug. Lei felt the comfort and strength of her friend's support, letting herself lean for a moment on Marcella. Then she stood back. "I need to find a dog-friendly place where I can keep Keiki. But in the meantime, I want to go see Consuelo's aunt, the one who took her and her father in when he was dying. Check if she's got any information, check the girl's room and see what we can find out there."

"When was she last home?" Lei asked the striking Filipina woman who'd identified herself as Sherrie Ilanoco, Consuelo's aunt.

"Consuelo's with her boyfriend. Is she in trouble? Consuelo's a good girl."

"I'm sure she is." Ken made a little patting gesture with this hand. "We have an investigation going on into something at Paradise Air, and we wanted to ask her a few questions."

"Oh, that place." Ms. Ilanoco's full lips all but pulled away from her teeth in disgust. "You cops stay investigating them? Come in, then. I answer your questions." She threw the door wide.

"Okay." Lei followed Ken inside, feeling conflicted about withholding the fact that Consuelo was in Tripler Hospital. If they told her right away, she'd rush off, and interviewing her would be much more difficult, not to mention searching Consuelo's room.

The front room was dim and cool, with a flatscreen TV that took up most of one wall. Vinyl couches made a deep V of seating, and a toddler played with a couple of plastic action figures in front of cartoons on the TV.

"My grandson." She gestured to the child, who looked up, big, dark eyes tracking them as they followed her into the kitchen. "I'm making pickled mango. You like?" The counter, old-fashioned Formica with metal edging, was piled with green mangoes in various stages of chopped dismemberment. The room was filled with the tang of vinegar and sweet of mango. Ms. Ilanoco went back to her mound of fruit, picking up a paring knife to run it over a mango, quartering it into quadrants.

"I love pickled mango," Lei said, and without another word Ms. Ilanoco opened a Ball jar filled with pale yellow spears packed into vinegary sauce. She dumped a portion on a plate and pushed it over toward them with a couple of forks. She and Ken exchanged a glance, and both of them picked up forks. Winning Mrs. Ilanoco's trust was easier with a fork in hand.

"I hate that airline—it stole my brother's life. Max Smiley, he one greedy *haole*." As the matron grew more agitated, her pidgin thickened and she practically spat the words. She grabbed one of the corners of mango skin and ripped it off the hard green fruit, tossing the leathery skins into a wastebasket half full of the fragrant remnants.

"Go on," Lei said, spearing a slice of pickled mango and taking a bite. It was delicious—soury-sweet, with a soft but firm texture. "How long did he work for them?" It was good to be able to verify Consuelo's story.

"He was with Paradise for twenty years, and he came here to my house to die. He couldn't go back to work. He lost everything paying his bills after he lost his health insurance. So Consuelo, she get nothing." Ms. Ilanoco set the mango she'd peeled on a board and employed a cleaver with such enthusiasm both Lei and Ken backed up a bit.

"So Consuelo—does she ever bring her boyfriend here? His name's Tyson, right?" Ken asked.

"I nevah like that boy." Not quite a confirmation that Tyson Rezents was Consuelo's boyfriend, but almost. The cleaver whacked the last of the mango meat off a pit the size of a child's fist. "I tell her no bring him around here."

"So you said she's with him," Lei prompted.

"That's what she said. She never came home the last couple weeks." Lei and Ken exchanged a glance over Ms. Ilanoco's bent dark head—this was why Consuelo was never reported missing. "She changed after my brother died—didn't want to go to school, gone all the time, not listening to me. I figured I let her go; she come back when she ready. She told me she was going stay with him, but she never packed up her stuff."

Ken took up the thread. "Does she have a car?"

"No. She get a job, though. She works for the Honolulu Surf. She work in the maintenance department there."

"She work there long?" Ken asked.

"Do you mind if I look around her room?" Lei saw an opportunity—Ken could keep Mrs. Ilanoco occupied.

Mrs. Ilanoco gestured with the knife. "Sure. Help yourself."

Lei went in the direction she'd indicated. A door led into the garage area converted to a bedroom. It was painted violet blue, with rag rugs over the cement floor, and the girl's bed was a twin, neatly made. Lei checked around in the drawers, on the desk—the usual teenaged girl places. Under the mattress, she hit pay dirt—a marble notebook.

Dear Diary read the first entry. She snapped the book shut and walked back into the kitchen, where Ken had finished off the pickled mango and Ms. Ilanoco had moved on to dissecting her third fruit. "Can we take this? Look through here for clues?"

Ms. Ilanoco set down the cleaver, turned away to rinse her hands in the deep china sink. She dried them on a cheesecloth towel as she turned back. Her mouth set in a line, deep grooves beside it hinting at grief and anger. "Clues to what?"

For the first time, she seemed to realize there was more going on than they'd told her, and Lei couldn't let the kind woman find out from the hospital or the lawyer. She took a deep breath, blew it out on a sigh. "Consuelo's actually in a lot of trouble. You'll be getting a call anytime now, from Tripler Hospital. She's in there under psychiatric care. The more you can tell us about what she's been into, what's been going on with her, the better."

Mrs. Ilanoco's face paled; then her lips tightened. "You didn't tell me this at first."

Ken's voice was soothing even as he shot Lei a narrowed glance—once again, she'd stepped out on her partner in an early disclosure. "Sometimes in an investigation, we need to see what a family member knows without disclosing everything. We're trying to get to the bottom of what's led Consuelo to the mental state she's in—she broke into some houses, stole some things."

Mrs. Ilanoco's hand clapped over her mouth. "Oh my God! Please, take the journal! I don't know nothing. That girl, she never been talking to me these last few months, since her father passed. I have to go see her!" She hustled them out of the house, thrusting a jar of pickled mango into Lei's hands as she did so.

Back at the Acura, Lei stowed the Ball jar of pickled mango in the webbing alongside the door. She placed an evidence-bagged plastic hairbrush for DNA and fingerprints in her crime kit, along with the marble notebook journal, which she slid into another bag. "I want to take this home to read tonight."

Both their cells toned at the same time, and Ken, behind the wheel, read his text first.

The face he turned toward hers was white with shock. "There's been another Bandit strike. It's at the original site—the Smiley estate. Waxman says it's a major explosion."

The drive back over the mountains for the second time that day was a blur to Lei. All she could think of was the older couple, their emotional faces, their heartfelt response to her plea for justice for Consuelo. Max's repentant words rang in her ears, and she could see Emmeline Smiley's steely eyes as she confronted her husband—and Angel, ears pricked, tucked under Emmeline's arm.

They saw smoke as they wove through the residential neighborhood down toward the Kaneohe Bay. Three of the FBI SUVs (one containing Gundersohn and Waxman) had pulled up into the driveway crowded with fire rescue vehicles.

The house Lei had left so recently was devastated. At least half of it was gone, splintered outward from an explosion. Smoke still billowed from the debris, and firefighters aimed hoses at the hole where the front door had been. Lei felt horror pinch her throat shut, black dots fluttering at the edges of her vision as she looked at what was left of the big beach mansion.

Chapter 23

*T*he Chinese dragons in the doorway were knocked sideways from the blast. Detritus, blown outward, formed mounds and piles that looked hazardous to navigate, sparkling with broken glass and twisted metal. Lei got out of the SUV, focusing on the stainless-steel door of the refrigerator lying directly in front of her, rows of condiments still held in place by a wire rack. There were two kinds of mustard, she noted—a Dijon in a glass pot and a plastic squirt bottle of bright yellow Heinz. She wondered which of the Smileys had preferred what kind of mustard.

Ken approached the police sergeant conferring with the fire chief in front of what would have been the entrance as the firefighters turned off the hoses. The ruin smoked sullenly as Lei picked her way carefully to stand behind him. "What's the status on loss of life?" he asked.

The police chief grimaced. "My men should be coming out any minute, but it looks like there were two casualties."

Lei walked to the edge of the shell of the house, trying to peer into the smoky interior. The fire chief put a cinder-streaked arm up to hold her back. "Your team can come in after we make sure it's under control and the remaining structure is stable," he said. "Stay back behind the line."

Where was Angel? It seemed impossible that something so tiny and fragile could have lived, and Lei felt ashamed to even be wondering about the dog when two people, people who'd showed signs of a real change of heart, were gone.

The "line" was a roll of fire hose that bisected the bluestone front steps. Lei rubbed her eyes, stinging with smoke, and tried to puzzle through what had happened.

Mere hours after she'd been at the lovely, peaceful home making her appeal to the Smileys, it was blown to smithereens and they were dead. Who could have done it? Consuelo was still in the hospital, and one of the other suspects, Rezents or Blackman, must have been occupied with the burglary of the Kahala house. Perhaps they'd split up? Or perhaps there was a new unsub at work?

The smells of wet charred wood, melted plastic, and smoke competed almost overwhelmingly, but her sensitive nostrils picked up a new scent that made her stomach flip inside out—the smell of cooked meat.

Lei turned and walked rapidly back into the driveway and around the undamaged side of the house toward the great steel barn, Max Smiley's toy chest—the place where it had all begun.

She made it as far as one of the clumps of bird-of-paradise before she bent over, heaving up the cup of coffee that was all she'd had that day. Every time she thought of the terrible burnt smell that must be either Max or Emmeline Smiley, she heaved again—and found her eyes stinging with tears as she did so, belly turning inside out and her emotions with it.

This was sick, and wrong, and horrible.

Whatever Consuelo had set in motion had taken a terrible new direction with her capture. Homeland Security would be the main player now, and this case had just gone from a courageous, idealistic, and misguided kid on a mission to domestic terrorism.

Rubber bullets wouldn't be used next time.

Lei felt something bump her leg, and she whirled, wiping her mouth with the back of her wrist, her hand on her weapon.

Angel looked up at her. She wagged the tiny curled whip of her tail. Her pointed ears were pricked, big brown eyes alight with happiness to see Lei.

"Oh my God." Lei scooped the dog into her arms and submitted to ministrations from the tiny pink tongue. "I can't believe you're alive."

Angel in her arms, she walked to the door of the steel barn, which was up, retracted into its channel. The unsub was probably long gone, but just in case, Lei took out her weapon and held it in one hand, the dog tucked under her arm, as she moved slowly into the interior, scanning. Spray paint haphazardly defaced the antique cars in their neat rows, and the hanging windsurfer sails were slashed. The chemical smell of spray paint was sharp in her nostrils—and she realized, belatedly, that it shouldn't be that fresh.

An engine screaming into life came from her left, amplified to the howl of a chain saw in the echoing steel space. One of the quads came roaring out of the corner, headed straight for her.

Lei fired a round at the black-suited, helmeted figure on the four-wheeled motorcycle bearing down on her—but it went wide as she dove out of the way, slamming into one of the antique cars, trying to protect Angel from being crushed as the quad just missed her, striking her leg as she bounced off the hood of an early-model Chevy truck.

She slammed onto her back on the cement floor, her head spinning from the impact. Angel was still clutched to her chest and the Glock was still in her hand. She heard the high-pitched roar of the vehicle flying out of the barn and across the grounds toward the beach.

Ken appeared at the doorway, weapon drawn. "Lei! You okay?"

"Yeah." Lei sucked in enough air to reply, and Ken disappeared, running in pursuit.

Marcella and Rogers appeared next. "Unsub headed to the beach," Lei said. Rogers took off, but Marcella ran over, helping Lei sit up with her back against the Chevy's tire. "You hit?"

"He grazed me on the leg with the quad." Lei let Angel down, but the little dog stayed beside her, shivering with fright. Marcella rolled up Lei's pants leg, taking a look at her calf. "Looks okay." She helped Lei stand. "I'm surprised he was still here. Did you get a look at him?"

"Not really. He was all in black with a helmet on. I hope they can run him down."

"I know they'll try. You have to tell Waxman you were here this morning."

"I know." Lei finally holstered the Glock. "I didn't see any signs of anything unusual this morning. Front gate was locked; I identified myself and Max Smiley let me in."

"We know from the other burglary that they didn't have much security, and the unsub could have got in off the beach."

"He sure knew about that." She gestured toward the beach. "And a quad can move pretty fast on sand."

"I see you found a friend. I wondered what happened to the dog."

"She seems to have nine lives." Lei picked Angel back up.

"Well, this isn't good. We've gone from burglaries with redistribution of goods to the poor to rampant destruction and murder."

"This. This must be the Smiley Mafia at work," Lei said. "It seems like Consuelo and Rezents were trying to make a statement, but I'm not sure this is what they were trying to start—it's such a different level and type of violence. Homeland is going to come down on this like an avalanche."

"We'll be lucky to pick up what's left of the case," Ken said glumly, returning with Rogers. Both agents were sweating and disheveled. "He got away. We did a BOLO already."

"Well, go put that dog in the SUV before Waxman sees it and makes you take it to the Humane Society," Marcella said as they reached the door of the barn and she spotted their boss and Gundersohn approaching. "We'll head him off."

Marcella, Ken, and Rogers strode toward Waxman, and Lei trotted in the other direction, going around the back side of the barn and back to the SUV. She set the little dog in the backseat and gave her a piece of what must have been Ken's breakfast burrito to keep her quiet, cracked the windows, and turned back to face whatever came next.

Chapter 24

Lei sat on her little couch many hours of a long, sad day later, the marble notebook in front of her. They'd gotten on the road, combing the neighborhood on foot and in their vehicles for the unsub on the quad—with no further trace after the vehicle's tracks disappeared up off the beach. She'd been able to come home and take a shower, washing off the stink of smoke and death, and the relief to smell nothing but Ivory soap on her hands was tremendous.

Their team needed to get to whatever information the diary held as soon as possible.

Still, she took a moment to eat the burrito she'd picked up at Taco Bell on the way home. The body was a machine, and hers had been running on empty for hours. Angel, also freshly washed, shivered beside her in an old beach towel Lei had wrapped her in. Lei had opened the sliders, and warm evening air blew over them, a natural hair dryer, scented with a little plumeria from the tree out back—an antidote to the smell of anarchy.

Time to find out whatever Consuelo had chosen to write down

about the Smiley Mafia. She opened the notebook and picked up the camera from her crime kit to photograph each page for the briefing that would doubtless come later.

Dear Diary,

We buried my father today.

I think he would have liked the funeral. My aunty cried a lot, and at least ten people came from work. There was good music from his favorite ukulele band. Father Sing was really articulate, talked a lot about how hardworking he was, what a kind, generous man and a loving father.

All true. At one time.

I blame the cancer, drunken drivers, and the airline for all that wasn't said in the eulogy—like how he got to be ninety-seven pounds and how he started hitting me and Aunty. How he called me a bitch and a whore when I tried to take care of his bedsores and change the ileo-stomy bag. How he cried at night and it sounded like cats fighting on a fence, and I started wearing earplugs because I was in the room with him, trying to sleep on a futon.

The room smelled like urine and rotten fruit that I never could find to get rid of. I wanted to just shoot him up with the morphine a dozen times, but when I loaded the syringe, I just couldn't do it.

The only time he was a little bit okay was when we watched movies. Willie Wonka and the Chocolate Factory was his favorite, the old version with the funny-looking Oompa Loompas. Like Charlie's grandparents in the movie, he made me get in bed with him to watch.

And I could do it, because for a little while we both

forgot how sick he was. We watched that movie twenty-seven times.

I know. I counted.

Dying can change people. It's changed me, that's for sure.

Lei photographed the entry on the last page, her heart aching for the young girl in the oversized scrubs she knew was lying on a molded plastic bed with no hard corners.

Dear Diary,

Something people don't seem to realize is how many of us it takes to make Hawaii paradise. An army of invisible people with vacuums, and hedge trimmers, and chef hats.

I'm a foot soldier in that army.

Daddy's funeral was three days ago and I'm back at work. I wear Carhartts. Even in the lightest fabric they make, it's hot, and I'm a sexless little Oompa Loompa in them, with my tool belt and billed hat. Lucky to have the job—even I know that. And thanks to Daddy, I know my way around both a splitter and a spanner.

It's the only thing he left me.

Maintenance Department pays about three times what being a maid would, another reason to sweat in my coverall. Aunty offered to get me in at the Sheraton doing rooms—she has cousins who work there—but I like maintenance better. Even the Carhartt is better than their outfits.

Oompa Loompas? Oh yeah. Only, the maids aren't sexless. They wear little fitted white dresses. Somehow, even when on a schedule of fifteen minutes per room (twenty max, if there's been puke and parties), they're

*supposed to look cute and keep that outfit clean. It's part
of the "ambiance" of the hotel, Aunty says.*

They get $8.50 an hour and work like dogs.

I'll take my hot Carhartts any day.

Dear Diary,

*The Boyfriend tried to cheer me up after work today.
It's been two weeks since Daddy died, and I'm apparently still not a happy camper. He picked me up in his
truck, took me to the beach. We went to Waikiki, the
part just past the dragon boats where locals like to
surf.*

*"You need to remember the good times." He gave
me blue-eye sincerity along with some carnations from
Foodland—Mainland flowers. I gave him some stink-eye
in return.*

*I unzipped out of the Carhartts in the passenger seat
of his truck. I just wear a jog bra and a pair of bike shorts
under it, and I could see by the way he was breathing
that it was getting to him. Good. I like to get to him. I
wriggled out of the Carhartts. He was looking out the
window, but I could tell by his lap something was going
on down there.*

"I want a cold drink. Get one for me."

*"What do you mean?" He blinked. He's adorable,
really cute for a haole boy, but not that bright.*

*"Go to the store and get me one. Steal it if you have
to." I took down my hair. I keep it in a braid wound up
in a bun under my hat, but it's long, goes past my butt. I
undo the braid, pull my fingers through it, fluff it over my
body like I don't know what I'm doing.*

*Black, shiny, and full of ripples, it's pretty. He got kind
of glazed looking, watching me, and got out of the truck*

and headed back toward the hotels. I kept busy getting myself in the mood. When he got back, he had my favorite drink, an ice-cold Monster, the sixteen-ounce size with the lid.

"Yay!" I drained half of it and then rewarded both of us. Beach towels rolled up into the tops of windows make a nice privacy tent.

I didn't feel invisible, at least for a little while. We'll see how long it lasts.

Dear Diary,

Called in sick and lay in bed all day. I'm sick all right—sick of life.

I could die back here and no one would notice. If I hold my hands up, I can see the veins in them, shadows under the skin hinting of the rivers inside. There are rivers inside me, black flowing passages leading to my heart.

How many days would it take for anyone to miss me? I imagine my blood filling the bed as I let that river out, soaking the mattress like a giant tampon. The smell, that fresh tingly iron smell, becoming a hot, sweet stink. Me swelling and turning colors and maggots filling my eyes.

Probably, with my luck, it would be my baby cousin coming in here that would find me, and the poor kid would be in therapy for life. I can't do that to the family. But this can't go on.

I need something to DO.

I want to be like the guy in Fight Club *who woke up to have everything taste amazing, like after Tyler held the gun to his head.*

It all tastes like sawdust now.

Dear Diary,

I'm spending more and more time at the Boyfriend's house. We lie on his mattress on the floor and watch Fight Club. *I think I have most of the lines memorized by now. This scene still stands out, where Tyler's steering down the wrong side of the road into traffic and says, "What did you want to do with your life?"*

Jack doesn't know, and as they are blazing into the headlights, he admits he doesn't know and he doesn't feel good about it.

Yeah. That's me. That's my life. I don't feel anything good about it.

I tried speed the other day; Sheila stole it from her ADHD brother and swore it would make me feel better. I just got hyper and cleaned the Boyfriend's whole damn place, and then I was pissed off because that was all I could think of to do with all that energy—clean that place.

So I took one of the Boyfriend's hoodies and went out and stole some shit from a store. But I didn't want it for myself. I don't need anything. All that energy, I went down to Ala Moana Park with a nice T-shirt and a pair of Reeboks I'd stuck in my pockets.

I gave the stuff to this homeless guy, and he smiled, and I wished I'd got him a toothbrush too. Maybe I'll do that next time. It felt a lot better than housecleaning made me feel, even than sex with the Boyfriend makes me feel.

Fight Club *is my gospel—and right now I'm redistributing wealth. Maybe that's what I need to do with my stupid little meaningless Oompa-Loompa life.*

Something big. Something amazing. Something totally fucked up.

Here's my symbol:

smiley face with hooked mouth

So that's where the smiley face came from. Lei got up and got a glass of water, staring sightlessly out the window at the lackluster view off her deck, absorbing what she'd read. Then she went back and took pictures of pages filled with smiley faces with their distinctive twisted mouth.

Consuelo had found her mission and her signature.

Dear Diary,

Daddy used to let me into the hangar when he was working on the planes. Under their swelling white bellies were secret panels that opened. I was reminded of the tonton in that Star Wars movie. All these guts are in there, and I was so small, he could boost me up inside and then, on his ladder, he'd show me everything he was doing as we checked all the parts and did a replacement of anything frayed, or broken, or burned out. He was on the Scheduled Maintenance crew, and after every three hundred hours of flight time, the plane would come in for a thorough work over.

If people knew how seriously Daddy took his job, how he'd hold up even a little fuse and frown at it like it committed a crime if it burnt out—they'd feel safer.

Mr. Smiley was always trying to get him to speed up, do more, fudge on replacement parts. The FAA had a quality-assurance list, and Daddy showed it to me—all the things on each model of plane that could be replaced to keep the plane in tiptop shape. But Mr. Smiley thought it was too "conservative" and told him to lie.

He wouldn't.

In the end, that's why I think Mr. Smiley wouldn't give him leave when he got sick. He'd already been writing him up for every little thing, trying to fire him. It makes

me so mad when I think about it—that man, with so
much, wouldn't let Daddy keep so little—his health care
and his job.

Dear Diary,

The Boyfriend and I drove out to Max Smiley's
Kaneohe estate—I'd found out the address by hanging around with that bigmouthed bitch Reynalda, who
seems to feel guilty for what happened to Daddy. It
wasn't hard to park the truck and walk down the beach
through the public access. The Boyfriend wondered why
I wanted to go to that particular beach, why I insisted
even.

I made him haul the towels, radio, and cooler all the
way down the beach, and we set up on the beach in front
of the Smileys' great big mansion.

I didn't tell him why, because I don't quite know why.
Yet. But I think Tyler Durden would know. I wish he were
real and would tell me what to do.

After the Boyfriend fell asleep in the sunshine, I
sneaked up onto the grounds. Nobody around, no security to speak of, and the door open on the most glorious
storage barn I'd ever seen.

I don't have my driver's license yet, but there are
a number of vehicles I wouldn't mind taking out for a
spin. My favorite is a tiny silver ultralight plane, as
classy a vehicle as a solid chrome Porsche, parked
right in the front facing the mini landing strip, begging
to take off. Daddy showed me the basics on flying, and
with a little Internet research, I'm sure I could figure
it out.

That's when the little dog came yapping up. I knelt
down behind a bush and tried to shush her. She's a Chi-

huahua with a Napoleon complex. That just made her madder, and she barked so hard, she flew up in the air on each bark: "Riff! Riff! Riff!"

Her little bat ears were down, and she looked kind of scary for a two-pound dog. She's brave, and I like that. I gave her a piece of mochi I had in the pocket of my shorts, and that shut her up chewing—and I made my getaway.

That tiny silver plane is some kind of sweet. Bet Max Smiley would miss it if it were gone.

Dear Diary,

I told the Boyfriend what I'm planning. He was pretty shocked, I could tell. "I need you for what I have in mind," I told him. "I can't do it without you."

He loves that stuff, really eats it up. Probably from having nobody care about him. So I'm not just doing it for me. I'm doing it for him and for all the people we'll help—the Oompa-Loompa army of have-nots that really run our islands.

He watched Fight Club with me again because I said we had to. Smiley Mafia is all in there—it's our Project Mayhem.

This time he seemed to get it, and he said, "We need someone to tell our story. We need people to get behind us, to try the one percent in the court of public opinion."

The reporter was his idea.

I'm not sure about her. She's got a sharp nose, and I can tell she doesn't care beyond the story. But the Boyfriend insists she can be useful and will help us in the end if we get caught. We're juveniles, at least, he says. He has a whole plan he's talking about—he calls it Plan B.

Plan B. That's the thing. I don't have one.
There's only Smiley Mafia.
smiley face

Lei set aside the last page of Consuelo's journal. She got up, paced around the apartment holding Angel. She wondered what Consuelo had been thinking, leaving the diary in such an easy place to find—maybe it was a sort of extended suicide note, because it was clear from the pages that she'd never planned to survive her stint as the Smiley Bandit.

The pages filled with round, precise, girlish handwriting drew Lei back. She picked up the camera. It was all here—the inspiration for the Smiley Mafia, the direction Consuelo's anger had taken and how it had morphed into a bold, suicidal series of burglaries. There was anger there, there was revenge—but there wasn't *murder.*

Someone had taken things in a different direction after Consuelo's capture. One of her conspirators, maybe the Boyfriend, was using Consuelo as a martyr, a figurehead.

Lei had to talk to the girl again, with the journal pages and pictures of the Smileys' bodies on the floor of the shell of their house in her hand.

That ought to jar the Smiley Bandit out of her catatonic state.

Chapter 25

*L*ei e-mailed the photos of the journal to all the team members and called to leave a message on Ken's voice mail on the way in to Tripler Hospital, relieved he hadn't picked up and insisted she attend some departmental briefing where they all rehashed what they knew and got assignments—she knew the drill by now, and it continued to annoy. The grilling Waxman had given her at the Smiley bomb site still smarted—she really didn't think there was more she could have done to stop the unsub's escape, and she considered herself lucky to just be walking with a limp.

Lei showed her badge and was admitted to Consuelo's room.

The girl was looking better, sitting upright and reading a celebrity magazine in the sunlight coming from the window. Lei glanced at the small, high aperture above the bed—wire threaded the glass, and there was no latch to open. In the closed space of the room, a smell of socks competed with burger cooking somewhere not far away. Lei thought this setting would drive her insane in less than a week.

"Hi, Consuelo." The girl looked up but didn't return the greeting. Lei set her phone, on Video Record, on a chair she dragged in from outside. She pointed the phone's recording eye at Consuelo and stated the date, time, and location. She remembered from the journal that many of Consuelo's deepest feelings were associated with movies, with the themes and stories they explored.

"So, is this feeling like a scene from *Girl, Interrupted*?" Lei asked, as she sat on the edge of the built-in bed, the journal in its evidence bag resting on her lap. "Glad to see you looking better."

Consuelo's eyes narrowed and flicked to the bag. "What's that?"

"You know what it is." Lei took the marbled school notebook out of the brown paper bag. "Found it under your bed at your aunty's."

"That's private," Consuelo said.

Lei shook her head. "You know this has gone well beyond that. I've got to tell you some stuff and show you some pictures."

Lei took crime-scene photos of out of where she'd tucked them in the marble notebook, quashing a momentary qualm about whether she was doing the right thing. She hadn't checked with Dr. Wilson, who'd very nicely asked her to, or her partner or Waxman—but if Lei could get Consuelo to talk, she might be able to get out of the hot water Waxman had her bubbling in. Something had to snap the girl out of her stubborn silence on the subject of the Smiley Mafia and the whereabouts of Rezents and Blackman.

"Some things have happened since you went in here." Lei started with the photos of the Kahala estate, spreading them in a fan in front of Consuelo. "We knew right away, looking at these, that someone with a totally different and much more destructive style was taking the movement you'd started in a new direction."

Consuelo looked at the photos of the home destruction without responding. Her long hair hid her face—but Lei saw her full mouth twitch, and she picked up of the photos of the spray-painted slogans and smiley-face logos with a slight grimace, quickly smoothed away.

"Smiley Mafia is meant to be a virus, to spread."

"Well, it has. And it's gone deadly." Lei laid a picture of the burnt, mutilated bodies of the Smileys, their clawed hands reaching for each other in a nest of ashes, on the bed in front of the girl.

Consuelo gasped, and her hand covered her mouth as her big, long-lashed eyes looked up from the horrific scene. "What—who is this?" she asked.

"Max Smiley and his wife, Emmeline. A bomb was planted in their house and went off only hours after I was there and returned Angel to them."

"Oh my God. Angel." Tears welled, spilled. The girl looked back down at the grisly photo.

Lei had already decided not to say anything about Angel being safely ensconced in her apartment until she'd gotten all the information she could out of the girl. After all, this case had crossed into the realm of a terrorist investigation, and Lei's interview was likely to be the kindliest the girl was in for. Ken had let her know that Homeland Security was going to be interviewing Consuelo, and Lei was glad to have beaten them to the hospital.

"It's bad, Consuelo. Please tell me where Rezents and Blackman are, what their roles are. Trust me. You'd rather talk to me about this than the guys from Homeland Security. They could come anytime, and I'm pretty sure Dr. Wilson won't be able to keep you protected in here—they're all about stopping domestic terrorism, which your case has become. If you tell me what you know and we are able to intervene, we can probably end this thing before it gets any worse for you—and for your friends."

Consuelo looked up at Lei. Inner conflict was revealed in the drawn line of her brows, the scrunched set of her mouth, the shine of tears in her dark eyes. "I never meant for anyone to die but me."

"I know." Lei reached out, clasped one of the girl's small, cold hands as it covered the gruesome photo. "I get it. I always did."

Consuelo told her all she knew, and Lei left the room working her phone.

Chapter 26

*L*ei was the last in line, hunched over in the dim light of evening, behind the Homeland Security and SWAT teams. Perspiration beaded up on her lip as her heart thundered inside the tightness of the boldly marked FBI vest. She wore a helmet with a face guard, too, and her FBI teammates, ahead of her, were anonymous in their gear. They were primed to move on the intel she'd brought in from Consuelo.

She hoped like hell the girl hadn't hung her out to dry.

They crouched in the alley of a run-down downtown building, the heat of the day's sunshine radiating from the stucco-covered cement beside Lei and increasing the sweat she felt collecting between her breasts. She held her Glock in the "down" position. Marcella's shapely backside was directly ahead of her, recognizable even in the anonymity of their navy uniforms. She scanned the area, eyes checking for movement, but the alley was empty except for their crouched forms. At the front of the abandoned building, another team was poised to breach the other door.

She focused on her breathing and lowering her heart rate: *In through the mouth, out through the nose. In through the mouth, out through the nose.*

Just when she didn't think she could stand the suspense another minute, the team leader gave the signal and two of the agents swung the door cannon. The metal-reinforced door smashed inward with a boom.

The SWAT team poured in, well-coordinated as a martial-arts drill, and Lei followed Marcella, Rogers, and Ken as they trailed the team, checking through the empty, abandoned warehouse for the door that led to a downstairs cellar—a room Rezents, Blackman, and Consuelo had used as their recording studio for the videos and as a secure headquarters.

Lei waited at the top of the stairs as the rattle of gunfire broke out going down. This was the protocol—Homeland was in charge and the FBI were just there to observe and support.

Another rattle of gunfire; then she heard a laconic, "Proceed."

She sidled down bare, run-down wooden stairs behind Marcella, the Glock a welcome and familiar weight that gave her eyes and hands a focus as her heart thundered in her ears, amplified by her helmet.

The floor of the cellar area looked like a frat house in a bad movie. Futons decorated the floors, and the video area was a chair in front of a black curtain tacked against the wall with a camera on a tripod pointed at it.

Tom Blackman lay sprawled on the ground, blood pooling beneath him, turned away from her with his arm extended and a pistol still in his hand. Lei recognized him from his photo, even with a beard shrouding his face. His dirty blond hair was longer, and his eyes were closed.

One of the Homeland agents kicked the pistol away while another knelt and felt for a pulse at his neck. He turned back to them, shaking his head.

"Damn." Marcella's voice came through the comm in the helmet. Lei could tell by the flatness of her tone that the agent's comment wasn't out of sympathy. The fact was, now they'd have no way to get any more information on the Smiley Mafia from Blackman.

Lei holstered her weapon. "Rezents?" she asked.

"No sign," the Homeland agent said.

One of the agents had been hit, and a few of his fellow officers were administering first aid. It looked like a shoulder wound, not serious. She could hear the cry of emergency response sirens, muffled but penetrating even to this underground bunker, scented with the tang of blood and an overnote of unwashed bodies and mildew.

Lei looked around at three futons in a row against the wall. There was one rumpled sleeping bag on one of them. Accumulated trash from packaged food overflowed a plastic bag, and a stack of pizza boxes towered against one wall, adding a twist of rotting food to the smells she was already battling.

Against another wall was a table littered with the detritus of bomb making—sticks of dynamite. A can of gunpowder. A jug of ammonia. Duct tape, sections of pipe, bags of nails.

Nothing good could come of such things.

Her heart sank for Consuelo—had she known this was where the Smiley Mafia movement was headed? Or had Blackman and Rezents been the ones to take it there? There was only one of them left to bring in, and hopefully the "virus" would be contained.

But even with Blackman dead at her feet, Lei had a bad feeling about it.

Chapter 27

*L*ei drove her Tacoma home along busy Ala Moana Boulevard through the cooling blue light of evening two days later. She realized she hadn't seen the ocean in days—in fact, ever since they'd chased down the Hummel, time seemed to have both speeded up to a blur and slowed down to a series of snapshots that was all her memory seemed able to maintain.

On impulse, she turned off onto the little side road that led to Waikiki Yacht Harbor.

Lei parked the truck near the breakwall, pulling up against the decrepit cement parapet. This public parking area was a holdout for locals, even in downtown Waikiki, and she watched surfers as the sun set behind the turquoise-blue waves peeling near the harbor jetty.

She hadn't slept well the last few days, those snatched dark hours between endless briefings, conference calls, and scrounging through the crime scenes for any prints or DNA that would tie their three suspects to the crime sites in Kahala and Kaneohe. Other than the comfort of Angel sleeping in her air mattress with her, curled up against the back of her neck, there wasn't anything in her life she was enjoying right now.

Lei actually missed the time in her career when a good day in law enforcement had been breaking up a bar scuffle, chasing down a purse snatcher, or ambushing a cockfight. The last few days, filled with interagency meetings and all the detail work of piecing together the case, had rendered the back of her neck stiff. A headache lingered at the base of her skull, and she hadn't had time to run since the Smiley Mafia debacle began.

On impulse she got out of the truck, stripped off her gun, badge, and shoes, rolled up her pant legs to the knee. She beeped the truck locked and walked down to the water, the sand massaging delightfully between her toes, the last of the setting sun gilding the coconut trees and rigging of the moored boats with ochre light. Dramatic cumulous clouds massed along the horizon, separating rays of sunset into bars of gold.

This was the Hawaii tourists came to experience—and it felt like another world entirely to Lei, shut up in a series of boxy air-conditioned rooms and crime scenes with nothing to look at but ugliness and bad smells.

The scent of the ocean, green and fresh, felt as good as a shower to her, the simple shush of the waves on the sand, a lullaby.

She sat in the sand, rubbing the coral and bits of shell back and forth against her feet, and propped her hands on her knees as she watched the sunset.

The Smiley Mafia movement continued, but seemed to be losing steam. The latest incursions had taken the form of graffiti and vandalism, and recent burglary attempts on several houses had been unsuccessful due to increased security.

The focus and intelligence that had marked the campaign as it began had dissipated—and so had the deadly turn it had taken.

Rezents was still at large, but Homeland suspected the disorganized gestures they'd been dealing with were done by copycats, followers, a few misguided kids looking for an excuse to act out against the obvious target of "the one percent."

Lei's phone vibrated a message reminder at her. She slid the phone out of her pocket and spotted three voice mails on it—Stevens, Alika Wolcott, and her grandfather, Soga Matsumoto. Her heart picked up speed.

She listened to her grandfather's voice mail first. He wanted to confirm their lunch—which she'd forgotten in all the drama with the case—and he concluded with "I've been thinking a lot about what you said." No further explanation. She wondered what he meant and noted the date of the lunch in her phone so she'd remember it.

The next message was Alika. "It brought up a lot seeing you at Women's Fight Club. I wonder if you want to get some coffee sometime." Oh God—did she want to open that door again? She was shocked he'd even give her another chance, and she honestly didn't know what she felt about it.

She saved Stevens's message for last.

"What's going on with the case? We hear a lot of rumors over here, and we're having some trouble with vandalism and graffiti with the Smiley Mafia symbol all over it. Wondering when you want me to come over and bring you your dog."

She closed her eyes and listened to Stevens's baritone voice talk to her again.

And again.

And again.

She couldn't go out with Alika while she was still doing shit like that. It just wasn't fair to the guy.

She texted Alika, just to get it over with: *Thanks for the invite to coffee, but I'm still in transition and I'm not dating for a while.*

At least she wasn't leaving him hanging.

Lei stood up, dusted off her pants, and headed for the truck. The phone in her hand rang, as if on cue. It was Ken.

"Special Agent Lei Texeira," Lei said automatically.

"Lei, get to a TV. Watanabe's on with Rezents. He's turning himself in."

Lei jumped into the truck. "I'm coming back to the office. Are you still at the Bureau, Ken?"

"No, I'm at home. Damn reporter—she called Waxman just as they were beginning the interview. Some of HPD's finest are on their way to arrest him, but he's going to have his fifteen minutes of fame."

Lei punched up KHIN-2 News on her phone. "I'll head back. I'm sure Waxman wants us to come in." She clicked off the phone and turned on her Bluetooth, listening to the broadcast and glancing down at the video as she headed back toward the FBI office.

Watanabe, brilliant in a cardinal-red suit, sat across from Tyson Rezents. The young man's brown hair was bisected by comb tracks and his cheeks were pink with nervousness and a recent shave. Wide blue eyes tracked nervously around the studio as he pleated his chinos with his fingertips. He looked handsome, sincere, and too impossibly young to be a terrorist bomber.

"Tell us about the Smiley Mafia," Watanabe said.

Rezents combed his fingers through his forelock, mussing the comb tracks. "The thing people need to know is that when Consuelo and I began the movement, we never meant for anyone to get hurt. We just wanted to draw attention to the imbalances here in Hawaii, to some people who take from our islands and don't give back, and some causes that need more resources." His earnest blue eyes stared into the camera with the hypnotized gaze of a rabbit at a snake.

Watanabe verbally nudged him. "So what was your plan?"

"Consuelo wanted to do a stunt. She felt like all these people in the service industry are like Oompa Loompas in that old *Willy Wonka and the Chocolate Factory* movie—seen but not heard, keeping everything pretty and running smoothly for all the off-islanders to enjoy. She was angry and grieving her dad's death, and she had this idea to embarrass Max Smiley and some of the one percent that just keep homes here.

"Anyway, it was all Consuelo's idea—at first. I was the one who brought Tom Blackman in. I knew him from work. He got fired from Paradise Air and he was mad at Max too. I asked him to help us out, to help with the videos, keep things going while Consuelo flew around and hit the targets. I didn't know he had his own agenda."

Rezents seemed to run down. He began plucking at his pants, and one of his knees bobbed. Sweat pearled on his forehead and upper lip. "He had a lot of ideas. Consuelo started her plan to launch Smiley Mafia—she flew off and left—and Blackman wouldn't listen to me. Once Consuelo was caught, he said Smiley Mafia needed to go viral and make change, and the only way to do that was with bombs. I think he was off in the head—crazy."

"Well." Watanabe gave Rezents a patronizing smile. "One might say the same of you and Consuelo. Couple of pretty crazy kids."

"Consuelo was sad and angry. I love her. I was doing this for her and because I believe in righting some inequalities. But neither of us would kill anybody!" Rezents's voice rang with conviction. "I tried to stop Tom with the bomb making and he threatened to kill me. I left the bunker after Consuelo was captured on Molokai—I took off. I was scared and hiding. I didn't know what to do. I couldn't believe it when I saw he'd blown up the Smileys!"

"So you didn't know he planned to do that?" A loud pounding, cries of "Open up!" penetrated the background, and Watanabe glanced off-camera before Rezents answered. "We don't have any more time, Tyson. Anything else you want to say?"

"I'm sorry we ever started this. People, if you're vandalizing and robbing houses for the Smiley Mafia, stop it. It's over. Consuelo's the only one who's a real hero, and she's..." Lei glanced down to see his expression on the tiny screen of the phone, and she could swear there were tears in his eyes, and the sight brought an answering prickle to her own. "She's really brave. She really cares about changing things."

The doors burst open, and two police officers rushed forward and horsed him out of the chair, hustling him out of the camera frame.

"And there you have it. Tyson Rezents, the young man behind Homeland Security and the FBI's massive manhunt, wanted in the murder of Paradise Air's owner Max Smiley and his wife, Emmeline, has turned himself in here on KHIN-2 and said his piece. It will be interesting from here on out to see how our domestic agencies make their case and who they blame for the ongoing vandalism going on across the islands by the movement calling itself Smiley Mafia."

Lei punched off the phone and concentrated on getting into the office. This was going to complicate the prosecution no end. Rezents had very effectively biased the jury pool in Hawaii—but at least he was now in custody. As things currently stood, they were having a hell of a time tying anyone but Blackman to the Smiley murder. She hoped Homeland had at least been able to tie the explosives at the last two sites to the materials found on the bench in the basement.

Once in the office, she joined Waxman and Ang in the conference room. "Good evening, sir," she said.

"Is that sand I see?" Waxman's eyes crinkled at the corners as he pointed to her shins—she'd forgotten to roll her pant legs back down, and her backup pair of rubber slippers were on her feet.

"Yes, I'm afraid it is." Lei pushed the pants down. "I listened to the broadcast on my phone after Ken called me."

"Well, we're backseat to Homeland now, so let's not bother rushing down to interview Rezents. We probably won't get access anyway. They're really focusing on the bombs and bomb making, and hopefully he has more to say about that than just blaming it all on Blackman. Agent Ang, can we watch the video again?"

"Yes, sir." They were doing that, with pauses to discuss how to support the prosecution's case, when Ken arrived.

Trailing in his wake was Barry Kleinman, attorney general for the city of Honolulu, a transplant to Hawaii back in the 1970s who still wore the beard and thick-lensed glasses he'd probably sported back then.

"We're going to need to block a change of venue for this case, for starters," Kleinman said. "I've been in touch with Homeland, and they've verified that the bomb-making materials found in the basement were used in the Smiley explosion—but not the vandalized estate in Kahala. So that was probably a copycat."

Lei listened as they discussed the building of the case and the changing role of the Bureau since the entry of Homeland. Tom Blackman's hands and clothes, tested at the morgue, were positive for explosives, and the missing quad had been found parked a block from the basement stronghold, making him a strong candidate as the bomber.

In contrast, Rezents appeared clean, the hourly motel where he'd been staying empty of anything but his sleeping bag and computer. Rezents insisted he'd left the basement and parted ways with Blackman the day Consuelo was captured and had just been trying to figure out how to turn himself during the intervening days, terrified as Blackman took the situation from bad to horrific.

"What about Consuelo Aguilar?" Lei asked. "What's happening to her?"

Kleinman's watery blue eyes blinked behind his thick lenses. "I thought you guys heard."

"Heard what?" Waxman asked, leaning forward.

"Dr. Wilson prepared a report recommending psychiatric care

and making a plea for "mitigated circumstances" for Consuelo as a minor. Bennie Fernandez and I met yesterday, and we're drafting a plea agreement."

"What is it?" Lei asked, her palms itchy with nerves. She still hated the thought of Consuelo behind bars.

"She's going to be in the hospital until Dr. Wilson says she's off suicide watch, and then she'll be transferred to Ko'olau Correctional Youth Facility to serve two years until age eighteen. She has mandatory counseling as part of her program, and she'll be able to complete her high school diploma there."

"That's very generous," Waxman said.

"Indeed it is. Girl's got such a fan base, it's been a balancing act to make sure she's getting consequences, but not more than the public will tolerate. Bennie Fernandez says he's been contacted by several Hollywood producers wanting permission to interview her and access to her story."

"It's a good story, as Wendy Watanabe well knows," Ken said.

"Maybe you could draft an agreement that profits from her story will pay back the damages to the houses robbed," Lei said.

Kleinman sat back in his padded chair, took off his glasses, cleaned them on the front of his tropical-print aloha shirt. "Not a bad idea, but the interesting thing about the owners Consuelo burgled is that they've all refused to press charges, and they've honored the donations she made in their names. So if the state department didn't press charges, there basically wouldn't be any. This has given us a lot of latitude, and her mental health situation, age, and gender are also factors. I feel satisfied with this plea agreement."

Lei held her breath, waiting for argument from the other agents, but even Waxman nodded and said, "I'm sure Rezents is a different story."

"Indeed he is. For one thing, the boy's seventeen, almost legal age. Right now I'm waiting for Homeland to show me a provable connection between him and the explosives. It seems incredible he didn't have a bigger role to play than Blackman, but as I said, there's still no physical evidence tying him to any of the other vandalized sites or to the Smiley murder." He slid his glasses on, blinked his eyes owlishly, and stood. "Just wanted to check in."

"Thank you for keeping us up-to-date." Waxman walked him to the door. After he escorted the attorney general out, he turned back to the agents. "I would say we're on track to wrapping this thing up. Everyone get home and get some sleep. Tomorrow we meet with Homeland and go over the case in detail."

Lei drove home in the dark to pick up Angel, hurrying to get to Tripler Hospital before visiting hours ended at eight. When she got to the adolescent unit, the nurse who admitted her told her Consuelo had had to be taken out of the dining room with the other kids. She'd cut her wrists—and had almost done some serious damage to herself, even with a plastic knife.

Lei found herself rubbing old scars of her own self-injury as she looked into the girl's room through the wire-bisected window. She reached into her pocket for her metal talisman. Consuelo was on the bed, turned against the wall, her long black hair snarled over the back of the plain gray sweats she wore. The nurse unlocked the door, and Lei carried in a chair from the hall.

Angel squirmed inside Lei's tucked-in shirt, and as soon as the nurse shut the door, she pulled the shirt out of her pants and let the little dog out, setting her on the cot with Consuelo. Angel clambered over the still form, snuffling and whimpering, licking the girl's cheek until Consuelo's eyes opened. She rolled over onto her back, her hands coming up to clasp the Chihuahua.

"Angel. Oh, thank God. I thought you'd died." Consuelo's tongue seemed thick, her eyes puffy and glazed with some kind of sedative, and Lei's heart squeezed at the sight of the fragile wrists covered in taped gauze.

Nothing seemed to matter but the reunion between Consuelo and Angel, and the girl eventually sat up, clasping the tiny dog to her chest. Angel continued to lick anything she could get her tongue on, and right now it was Consuelo's neck as the girl looked at Lei. "How did you get her in here?"

"My shirt." Lei grinned. "She seemed to know something was up. She was really quiet until we got in here, and she smelled you."

"Where are they keeping her?"

"I have her, actually. And I wanted to tell you, things are looking very good for you. I heard only two years in Ko'olau, therapy, and you get to finish high school."

Consuelo lowered the fan of her long lashes, rubbing Angel's belly. "Two years feels like forever."

"I'll keep Angel for you. You can have her back when you get out. I've checked, and the Smileys didn't have any children or family who wanted her. If I hadn't taken her, she'd have gone to the Humane Society."

Consuelo looked up. Something new glimmered in those dulled dark eyes—Lei thought it might be hope. "Really? I can have her back?"

"That's the plan," Lei said stoutly. She'd already begun perusing ads for a cottage or ohana unit so Stevens could bring Keiki over, and she smiled to think of the big Rottweiler and the tiny teacup Chihuahua, with their matching markings, side by side. "What do you think of the therapy here?"

"Dr. Wilson's all right. She's the only one I've seen. But I think therapy's lame."

"I know you're a *Fight Club* fan. Just think if Jack had been able to—well—realize sooner that he was also Tyler Durden." Lei had rented the film and watched it twice, hoping to understand Consuelo's take on it. "If he'd been able to be more his whole self, make smaller changes in his life, he wouldn't have had to kill Tyler to keep him from taking over in the end. Jack really needed therapy, and all those visits to the cancer groups and such were him trying to get it without really getting it."

Consuelo petted the little dog, long, slow strokes, and Angel went limp, eyes closed in bliss, draped over the girl's leg. "I don't know."

Lei pushed up her sleeve, extended her arm to Consuelo. Thin white lines of old scar tissue, stacks of them, marked the pale skin of her inner wrists, marching up to her elbow.

"I know what pain feels like. I know what cutting does. And I know what therapy can do. Dr. Wilson was my therapist, too, back in the day." Consuelo's eyes widened as Lei pushed up her other sleeve and showed her the other arm. "I know what it is to want to die and also to want to live. I never want to go back to this. I go to therapy when I need to, so I'll never cut again."

"Wow. That's really messed up." And for the first time, Consuelo sounded like just another sixteen-year-old.

Lei rolled her plain white FBI shirtsleeves back down and buttoned the cuffs. "You're the first person I've ever showed these to, other than my boyfriend. Give Dr. Wilson a chance, and just know Angel will be waiting for you when you get out. We'll visit as often as we can."

"Okay. But please don't go yet."

Lei stayed until the nurse came back and caught them with Angel. Lei's pleas got the dog admitted to the visiting list subject to Dr. Wilson's approval, which Lei was sure would be granted.

When they left, Consuelo smiled and waved goodbye.

Chapter 28

*L*ei scooped up saimin noodles with her chopsticks at the
noodle house her grandfather had chosen. He sat across from
her, slicing chicken katsu with a knife and fork before picking it
up with chopsticks, dipping the thin, deep-fried chicken strip into
sauce and bringing it to his mouth.

Soga Matsumoto was a small, wiry man with buzz-cut silver
hair and a square face that still hinted at handsome. His hands
were gnarled with arthritis and spotted from the sun. Lei could
see calluses in their palms and a rim of dirt he'd failed to scrub
out from under a fingernail.

Conversation had been stilted, interspersed with covert obser-
vations of each other. Lei kept looking for something about him
she recognized, anything that would remind her of herself or of
the memories she had of her mother, but with his hooded eyes,
lids sagging in a smooth fold over diamond-bright darkness, deep
grooves beside his narrow mouth, nothing about him looked or
felt familiar.

"Do you garden?" She gestured with her chopsticks to his
hands.

"Yes. In fact, I'd like to show you the garden. I have bonsai trees. I sell them to a nursery. Sometime, maybe, you can come see."

"That sounds nice." Lei chased more noodles around. "Do we have any other family here I should know?"

"I have a sister. She has some grandkids around your age. But I think they've gone to the Mainland." Another precise cut of the katsu. "What are you doing for the holidays?"

Lei sensed there was a world of thought in the casually phrased question. "Actually, my dad and Aunty Rosario are coming over. Maybe we can all get together."

"Maybe." He chewed deliberately, swallowed. "I told you I was thinking about what you told me before, about the Kwon murder. I think you should stay out of it, let sleeping dogs lie."

Lei was surprised he brought it up. "That's what I've been doing—but I worry it will come back on me. Now I'm starting to want to know who did it—not just to clear myself but to solve it."

"Leave it alone. That's all," Soga repeated, clipping off the end of the sentence in a way that told her he wasn't going to say more. "On Memorial Day we have a lantern-lighting ceremony to remember the ones we've lost. We set the lanterns floating down on the ocean in Waikiki. I will be lighting one for your grandmother and your mother. It's in the spring, but I wonder if you'd like to come."

"Of course," Lei said, still wondering about his earlier comments. Surely this dignified older man who grew bonsai trees and made paper lanterns wasn't Kwon's shooter. "The festival sounds great." She'd seen pictures of the annual festival—thousands of paper lanterns floating on the sea, a tapestry of light, until they eventually burned out and were retrieved. "I've never seen it, but I've heard it's beautiful. I would love to remember them that way. I have a friend I'd like to make a lantern for." Mary Gomes, her friend on the Big Island killed some years ago, would always be in her heart.

Her grandfather told her he was a volunteer with the Shinnyo Buddhist temple that organized the event, and for months in advance he helped rebuild and repair the lanterns from the year before as well as making new ones. They discussed making the lanterns, and he invited her to come volunteer. They set a time for Lei to see his bonsai nursery, and when Lei left the run-down little noodle house, she felt as close to happy as she'd been since moving to Honolulu.

He might not look familiar, but on some level she knew him, and it was going to be interesting to get to know her neglected Japanese heritage a little bit.

She had family here, on Oahu.

Lei had asked that Ken sit in on her administrative conference with SAC Waxman, and it was allowed, to her relief. She took comfort from Ken's quiet strength beside her as he faced Waxman with her. The branch chief sat across from them in the conference room, Lei's file open in front and a pair of square steel reading glasses resting on his blade of a nose.

"I assume you know why we're here." Waxman looked at her over the glasses. Not for the first time, she noticed the cold intelligence of his gaze.

"I have some idea, yes, sir." Lei had returned to the office after lunch with her grandfather to find a message summoning her.

"Now that things are settling on the case, I need to do some cleanup. I'm officially notifying you of two negative reviews in your personnel file." Waxman showed her the Notice of Administrative Conference notice, holding it up. "You can ask for a union representative to attend this meeting, or waive that right."

"I waive that right," Lei said, steadying her voice. She slid her hand into her pocket to touch the white-gold disc.

"Sign here, then." Waxman pushed the paper and an FBI ball-point over to her. She picked up the pen and signed the paper, her hands prickling with sweat. She pushed the paper back to him. "Okay, on to the notes in your file. The first one is here: unpro-fessional representation of the FBI to the media. Initial that you have been informed. You may appeal the particulars of the note if you disagree."

Lei scanned the paragraph documenting her bungled interview with Watanabe, with a side note about disclosing confidential information—namely that the unsub was armed. She initialed the box beside the write-up, and Waxman went on.

"The other corrective note is for failing to follow Bureau pro-tocols on an investigation." Lei scanned two paragraphs there, documenting incidents of lack of communication, unauthorized interview of a witness/victim (her visit to the Smileys on the day of the bombing) unauthorized exit of an aircraft while in motion (jumping out of the helicopter), and unsanctioned disclosures to a suspect (content of her talks with Consuelo).

Of the details of these, the only one she felt was unfair was the disclosures to Consuelo—she'd been mandated to get informa-tion from the girl, but not allowed to give Consuelo any—and hadn't been informed of that.

Her hand paused by the initial box as she considered appealing that one—and then she signed.

If Waxman knew she was not only still visiting Consuelo, but she was holding the girl's dog for her, he'd add another whole paragraph on conduct unbecoming an FBI agent.

"Good. I'm glad you aren't fighting me on this." Waxman pulled the documents back and put them in the folder.

"Sir, I think we should strike the part about disclosures to a witness," Ken said. "You told her to get information out of Con-suelo Aguilar, and you provided no direction how you wanted that done."

"Ken." Waxman removed his glasses and made a steeple of his fingers. "I didn't let you sit in on the meeting as her union advocate. I let you sit in so you could bear some responsibility for the actions this young, green agent I assigned to you to has committed under your guidance. I think I'm going light on Texeira. One more note in her file—and I could easily generate one—and she'd be out of the Bureau for good since she's in her first year as an agent. I'm going light on her because I see what you see—Lei Texeira has talent as an investigator. Good instincts."

"So could you add a note in her file to that effect?" Ken asked, his face as serious as Lei had ever seen it. "I think she's more than earned that, even if the methods have been a little unconventional."

Waxman stared at them both for a long moment, then put his glasses back on. "All right." He used the ballpoint to write, "*Lei Texeira possesses the physical courage, initiative, and perseverance necessary in a federal agent as evidenced by her effective work resulting in the capture of the Smiley Bandit.*"

Lei initialed the box beside the handwritten note, her heart swelling with gratitude toward Ken. She sneaked a glance at him and could have sworn he winked, but it was gone before she could be sure.

"Agent Texeira, you're on probation for another sixty days. You'll be assisting Greg at the front desk and the other agents in whatever capacity they see fit, including coffee. Dismissed."

"Thank you, sir," Lei said, and shook his dry, cool hand before they left the room.

Back at their cubicle, she turned to Ken. "Thanks, partner."

"It was nothing." He flapped a hand.

"It wasn't nothing. Waxman's a hardass, but he even eked out a compliment because you asked him to. I know I've been a pain, but I want you to know I've enjoyed working with you and learned a lot from it."

"We'll work together again. In the meantime, can you get me some coffee?" He kept his face deadpan.

"Sure." She kept hers the same. "Cream or sugar?"

"With a side of humble pie." This time he definitely winked.

"I deserve it," Lei said. "Anyway. Thanks again."

"I'll take cream in my coffee," he said to her retreating back.

Three weeks later, Lei woke up in her new rental cottage and swung her legs out of bed. She'd hung her Glock in its holster from the scrollwork headboard where it was near to hand. Her phone was neatly plugged into the charger and rested on the bedside table along with the white-gold disc and her shiny FBI badge. She'd already bought a set of carpeted doggie stairs, and Angel hopped self-importantly down from the ratty beach towel at the foot of the bed where she slept.

Everything was in its place and finally ready.

Lei felt anticipation hum along her veins. Stevens was bringing Keiki home today. She got into the shower. Keiki brought good into her life, and she couldn't wait to see her dog again— and Stevens, too, however briefly.

Lathering up her curls, she mulled over the results of her administrative meeting with Waxman. Lei was still officially on probation, with Ken appointed her babysitter, and had been spending a lot of time running background checks and helping Greg in the reception booth.

Homeland Security had interviewed her about her visit to the Smiley house prior to the bombing, and her disclosures had resulted in an investigation as to her purpose in visiting the estate and even accusations that she might be a rogue agent who'd had something to do with the explosion.

Fortunately, that nonsense had eventually died down, but it hadn't been pleasant while it lasted. The whole series of events had left her in a tenuous position at the Bureau, and she shuddered to think of what Waxman would make of her secretly keeping Angel and the weekly visits to Consuelo, now beginning her sentence at Ko'olau Youth Correctional Center.

But at the moment, she didn't even care—Keiki was all that mattered. She turned off the shower, got out and dressed, indecisive—regular jeans? Or the nice skinny black ones? It was Saturday and she didn't have work, so she pulled on the black ones and a tight black tank that showed off her arms. She scrunched Curl Tamer into her curls. A whisk of mascara and a swipe of lip gloss, and she was ready. The doorbell set in the outer gate buzzed.

Stevens and Keiki were here.

Chapter 29

ei opened the door and stepped out onto the little porch. She held Angel tucked under her arm as Stevens unlatched the gate of the six-foot privacy fence that ran around the yard.

"Hey, girl!" Lei greeted the big Rottweiler whose leash he held. Angel's ruff rose against her arm, and the little dog emitted a series of high, aggressive yaps.

"This is her territory," Lei said as they approached. "They have to get used to each other." She set the Chihuahua on the ground and went forward to greet Keiki, whose hind end was doing a hula as the big dog whimpered with happiness.

Lei knelt, and Keiki sat. Stevens unclipped the leash, and Lei rubbed the dog's wide chest and submitted to a few tongue swipes, embracing the dog's sturdy neck, inhaling her scent—the Rottie smelled of coconut dog shampoo. Stevens must have washed her for the occasion.

Beside them, Angel barked so hard she flew up off the ground on rigid legs—"*Riff! Riff! Riff!*"

"I don't know if they're going to get along," Stevens said.

"Give them a minute," Lei said. Keiki stood back up, walked

over to the hysterical Chihuahua, and leaned down to sniff her. The tiny dog's ears flattened, her tail sank, and she ran behind Lei. Lei ordered Keiki to lie down to expose her belly to Angel's sniffing investigation, submitting patiently to this inferior creature's curiosity with a snort—a big-dog version of an eye roll.

Mutual sniffing achieved, the two dogs walked off to scent mark the yard.

"Thanks for bringing her back." Lei was unsure of how to proceed—hug him? Shake hands? Awkward standing, hands in pockets as they watched the dogs, might have continued if she hadn't gestured to the iron security door. It was the first thing she'd installed upon moving in. "Come in. Let me give you a beer, at least."

Stevens looked terrible. His clothes hung on his tall, rangy frame. He'd made some effort to clean up, she could see, because his cheeks were chapped by a recent shave. His hair was tousled and overlong.

Lei noticed, as she'd noticed before, that he looked good haggard—somehow it made him even more attractive. His sky eyes, flecked with white like ice in a Nordic lake, were even bluer with shadows beneath. She longed to comfort him, run her hands through that rumpled hair, massage the tension out of his corded shoulders. She wondered what was wrong and figured he'd get around to telling her—he always had.

"Corona?" She took a beer out of the fridge, popped the top, and handed one to him without waiting for a reply. It dangled from his fingers as he turned, taking in the bright, tidy kitchen with an orchid plant over the sink. The room was painted a cheerful yellow, and they sat at a small round table with a couple of chairs.

"Nice place."

She shrugged. "It came furnished. I learned my lesson after my last place. What a hole. Glad you never saw that one, or you might have thought I was depressed." She laughed a little too loud and drowned the discordant sound with a sip of her beer. "So how's Maui?"

"Same old, same old." Stevens's eyes had wandered to the bedroom. She'd finally replaced her prized king-sized bed lost in the fire on Maui, and the new one was dressed in plump pillows and a comforter. Lei wished she could get up and close the door. She felt as exposed as if he'd glimpsed her panties—thank God he'd never seen that other bed, the sad little inflatable mattress and nest of blankets she'd lived in too long.

"What's happening with the case? We haven't had much news about it over on Maui." He turned away from the bed in his line of sight. They'd always been able to talk about work, so Lei was relieved to move on to this neutral topic.

"Well, Homeland has failed to find any physical evidence to tie Tyson Rezents to the Smiley murders, so that's sticking to Blackman until something else pops. They've charged Rezents with conspiracy to commit terrorism, and he didn't get the good lawyer Consuelo did—but Watanabe's defense fund did get a competent guy at least, whose first move was a change of venue. His trial's been moved to Arizona, where they're hoping no one's too familiar with the case. But with the Internet celebrity of those kids, I'm not holding my breath. It's too bad Blackman went down in the raid. I would have loved to hear what he had to say about Smiley Mafia, which Consuelo started as a kind of idealistic *Fight Club*–inspired Robin Hood gig."

"That's sure not what it's become." Stevens leaned back in the kitchen chair to roll the beer bottle back and forth across his lean stomach. "We're cleaning up Smiley Mafia graffiti and vandalism every damn day."

"Yeah, same here. But there's no centralized intelligence to it anymore. It's just kids finding an excuse to trash stuff, like angry kids have been doing forever." Lei took a sip from her bottle as the dog door, intentionally large enough for the big Rottweiler, burst open, admitting Keiki and her tiny shadow, Angel.

Lei got up, called the dogs over to a pair of dishes next to the counter—one large, one small. The dogs put their noses down and ate side by side—and they looked as funny together as she'd thought they would.

Stevens grinned, and she smiled back at him.

"So, you can come visit Keiki anytime." Lei felt like one half of a divorced couple, offering visiting rights.

"I don't know. It's hard." Stevens took his first swig of beer, reached in his pocket and pulled out a ragged piece of paper. Turned to the table, opened its frayed folds. Smoothed it flat. "I have something to read to you. She said I could."

Lei's heart jumped to trip-hammer speed. "She" had to be Anchara. Stevens cleared his throat as if he were going to read the letter aloud, but then didn't, just staring down at the paper in his hands.

"May I?" Lei whispered.

He handed it to her, and she opened it, reading silently. Anchara's handwriting had a curly, unusual quality to it, attesting to her foreign schooling—but it was beautifully, cruelly, unforgettably legible.

Dear Michael,

(You may share this with Lei if you like, so there are no secrets between us. I always liked her, even when I wished I didn't.)

I appreciate all you tried to do for me. No one could have had a truer, better friend and gentler lover. You said you'd do your best to be a good husband to me, and you did try.

I know how hard you tried, always so thoughtful, and careful, and kind. But ever since you heard from her, I've seen the torment you try to hide from me. I know again how much you loved her—I saw it from the first—and how you were trying to get over her by being with me.

Well, it's not enough. We both deserve better.

I deserve to be loved for me. I'm strong enough to know that now, and I would rather be alone than settle for crumbs from the table of your love for her.

I've settled for others choosing my fate for me my whole life. It ends now.

When we fulfill two years, I'll divorce you. But I need to stay in this country. I need this green card, and we need to be married for those two years for me to keep that. For all I've done, all that's been done to me, I've earned that at least.

I don't love you. I haven't let myself. But I could have.

Anchara

Lei folded the letter, slid it back to him. Picked up her beer, walked to the sink, staring out the little window. Drank it down past the hard lump in her throat that held tears for the pain they'd all been through.

Pain they'd each caused each other. Pain she'd felt every lonely night without him and now an inner conflict and sorrow that his marriage wasn't working. Regret really did come in all sorts of shades and intensities. She could've done without the discovery of that. She turned back to him when she was pretty sure she'd blinked her eyes clear.

"I'm really sorry. It seems like you both wanted it to work."

"Yes. Yes, we both tried." He leaned forward, his elbows on his knees, rolling the empty bottle between his palms, a familiar movement.

Lei glimpsed the tiny purple heart with her name on it inside the crook of his elbow. He hadn't lasered it off. The sight of that, more than anything, made her walk over to him, lay her hand on his shoulder. Hesitant. Shy. Conflicted. But reaching out her hand, nonetheless.

"I sometimes wish I'd never left Maui. The FBI—it's not what I thought. I—don't know what to do anymore."

"I don't know either." He put the bottle down, and his long, hard arms wrapped around her waist, pulling her close against his face. Lei felt him shaking, his face pressed into her T-shirt. Her arms stroked his back, comforting, even as her heart ached—he was crying for having lost Anchara, and yet she felt nothing but love for him and sorrow for his pain.

This depth of feeling, this complexity of love, was entirely new to her. Lei felt it bloom in the exact place where his tears wet her belly, felt it tighten around her heart as his arms wrapped around her waist.

"I didn't want to love you. I tried so hard not to," he said, his voice rough as she stroked his hair.

"I know." And in a moment, she was in his lap, a familiar comfort, one of her favorite places in the world. The kiss they shared was messy with tears and longing.

She wondered how she'd done without him, how she'd continue to—and yet she'd never felt stronger.

"We can wait." Lei said it, sitting in his lap, holding his drawn face in her hands, his blue, blue eyes gazing into her brown. "We owe her that. Go home to Maui. And know I'll be waiting for you."

Acknowledgements

Broken Ferns was Lei's "dark night of the soul." This was a hard book to write.

I struggled, and sweated, and tore *Ferns* apart several times. I took breaks to write two other novels. I was so enamored with Consuelo and her story, I wrote entire chapters from her point of view, and then realized it gave too much away and I had to take it all out (a little book of Consuelo outtakes would be fun to do! She's an amazing character!)

I knew Lei needed to suffer, and grow, and learn to love unselfishly, and take chances not just with her physical self but in connecting with others. Over the course of these four books, my intention was to show one woman's path to healing from childhood sexual abuse—a terrible crime perpetrated every day, in way too many homes.

Childhood sexual abuse is not easily overcome. It often results in low self-esteem, leading to abusive adult relationships (perpetuating the cycle) or to an inability to trust and connect/commit to others. Lei has not always been likeable, even to me—but she's been consistent—physically brave, intuitive, driven, honest, unself-conscious. In this book, when she begins to become more self-reflective, to understand that her actions have consequences—I finally began to really like her. I hope you did too.

Lei's becoming a true hero—someone who overcomes both within and without, and sacrifices for the good of others.

There's more ahead. I hope you'll hang in there for the journey.

This is the first book my detective friend Jay Allen didn't have time to read—and I don't have any connections in the FBI, so I relied heavily on several FBI books and numerous Internet searches to develop my FBI world, and it's probably riddled with errors. I apologize in advance, and plead that this is a work of fiction, and a good story is the most important thing.

Thanks goes first to Holly Robinson, you were an incredible writing partner in that last leg. Your creative fire boosted my rockets to *get'er done*! And then, you did such an amazing analysis on the manuscript that it really deepened the characters—"we want to be in her head more!" was your challenge, and I took it. Thank you for your amazing friendship and generous sharing of your time and talent.

Thanks to my awesome beta readers Bonny Ponting and Noelle Pierce. I took virtually all of your advice and worked it in, especially to "make Lei really suffer over Stevens!"

Thanks always to my wonderful book production team: editor Kristen Weber, copyeditor Penina Lopez, book designer Linda Nagata, cover designer Julie Metz, and my talented husband Mike Neal who photographed a forest of ferns before we got our shot. Thanks also to all my wonderful Facebook friends and writing community who helped me find a name for Consuelo's anarchy movement. Let's keep making great books together!

Thanks to all the many wonderful fans who clamored for this book and reviewed the Lei Crime Series on Amazon, B & N and Goodreads. You told friends about the books and made them the success they are. Without you, I might never have dug deep and found the motivation to finish this difficult book.

And thanks be to God, who deserves all the glory.

Much aloha,
Toby Neal, February 2013

Look For These Titles In
The Lei Crime Series

Blood Orchids *(book 1)*

Torch Ginger *(book 2)*

Black Jasmine *(book 3)*

Broken Ferns *(book 4)*

Twisted Vines *(book 5)*

Companion Series Books:

Stolen in Paradise: *a Marcella Scott Romantic Suspense*

Unsound: *a Dr. Wilson psychological suspense*

Middle Grade/Young Adult:

Aumakua: Water Dragon, *a survival novel*

Sign up for email updates on new releases at
TobyNeal.net

CPSIA information can be obtained at www.ICGtesting.com
Printed in the USA
LVOW06s1923071015

457334LV00004B/109/P

9 780983 952497